STRINGS
Attached

STRINGS
Attached

Diane Dakers

ORCA BOOK PUBLISHERS

Library and Archives Canada Cataloguing in Publication

Dakers, Diane, author
Strings attached / Diane Dakers.
(Orca limelights)

Issued in print and electronic formats.
ISBN 978-1-4598-0970-3 (paperback).—ISBN 978-1-4598-1068-6 (pdf).—
ISBN 978-1-4598-1069-3 (epub)

I. Title. II. Series: Orca limelights
PS8607.A43S77 2017   jC813'.6   C2016-904478-5
                                      C2016-904479-3

First published in the United States, 2017
Library of Congress Control Number: 2016949048

Summary: In this high-interest novel for teen readers, Brielle steps into the
role of principal cellist when her best friend is injured.

Orca Book Publishers is dedicated to preserving the environment and has printed
this book on Forest Stewardship Council® certified paper.

Orca Book Publishers gratefully acknowledges the support for
its publishing programs provided by the following agencies:
the Government of Canada through the Canada Book Fund and the
Canada Council for the Arts, and the Province of British Columbia
through the BC Arts Council and the Book Publishing Tax Credit.

Cover design by Rachel Page
Cover photography by iStock.com

ORCA BOOK PUBLISHERS
www.orcabook.com

Printed and bound in Canada.

20 19 18 17 • 4 3 2 1

*To my brother Jeff, who played double bass
behind me but never poked me in the
back with his bow.*

One

I love Tchaikovsky.

I know that's a bit dorky. Okay, it's *supremely* dorky that my favorite tunes were written by a Russian guy in the 1800s. I know I should say that my favorite music is by Katy Perry. Or Lady Gaga. Or One Direction. Believe it or not, we play their music too. But let's face it. "Teenage Dream" and "Born This Way" don't sound all that exciting when they're played by a youth orchestra.

And the cello parts are usually lame. Sometimes I wish I played one of the cool instruments. Trumpet. Saxophone. Even violins get to play the lead parts. But nobody writes pop songs for the cello.

But Tchaikovsky. He knew how to write a line of cello music. The best one is *Marche Slave*.

The cellos open it. *Ba-da-da-dum. Ba-da-da-dum. Ba-da-da-dum-dum-dum-dum-ba-da-da-dum-dum-dum.* Then the violins come in, all whiny and eerie. We switch to pizzicato. That means we pluck the strings with our fingers instead of sliding the bow across the strings. The music builds, and we, the cellos and basses, play in syncopation—off the beat.

Gives me chills every time. I know, right? Dorky.

When we finish playing *Marche Slave* in rehearsal this afternoon, I will everyone to stay quiet and still. I want to savor the final notes as they float through the auditorium.

"Great job, everyone." Mr. Holmes, the orchestra conductor, wrecks the moment. "Let's take fifteen."

I lay my cello on its side and loosen the horse-hair on my bow. I stand up and stretch. I place the bow on the music stand I share with Tawni. She's my BFF—and she should be here by now. She said she was going to be late because of a big gymnastics meet. But the competition must have ended an hour ago. It doesn't take that long to get to the rehearsal hall from the gym.

Tawni plays principal cello. She's the best of the six of us in the cello section. I play second cello, so I sit to Tawni's right. That's the way it's been since we started playing cello together in fourth grade.

First we played in our elementary-school strings program. Then we played in the middle-school orchestra. Now we're in our high-school orchestra. We also play in this orchestra, the intermediate City Youth Orchestra.

Musicians from all over town audition for this group. Tawni and I auditioned together when we were twelve. Three cellists moved up to senior orchestra that year, leaving three openings. Tawni and I got two of them.

Not only that, but we immediately became the youngest first and second cellists ever to play in the CYO! The fourteen- and fifteen-year-olds were choked. They figured they would automatically be promoted within the cello section when the others left. They didn't count on us "little kids," as they called us, coming along. They had to admit pretty quickly, though, that we deserved the top jobs.

Ever since then, it's been Tawni and me, always first and second. This year we have a new third cellist. Colby just moved here. He's fifteen, a year older than we are, and he goes to a different high school. That's one of the great things about playing in this orchestra—we meet kids from all over the city.

Ella, our sixth cellist, is also new this year. She's only twelve, but she's pretty good. She'll move up quickly. Grant and Jaron sit beside her in the back row. They're both sixteen, so this is their last year in intermediate orchestra.

No way Jaron will get accepted into senior orchestra. He's too lazy and annoying. Grant has a shot at it. He's a solid player and a reliable, quiet guy.

"You should be principal cello," Colby says to me during our break today. "You're just as good as Tawni. And *you* never miss rehearsals."

I blush and look at Tawni's empty chair beside me at the front of the stage. I sit between Tawni and Colby. "I actually like playing second," I tell him. "I don't want to sit right at the front of the orchestra. I like having Tawni between me and the audience."

"Seriously? You never think about it? You never dream of being principal cellist? Don't you think it would be brilliant to be in that top spot, knowing you're the best in the band?"

I lower my voice. "Well, it has been kind of fun today, playing first chair. I mean, I'm still sitting in the second chair, but first chair is empty, so I'm sort of playing first today."

Colby looks confused. My words don't always come out right when I talk to him.

"Come on, Brielle." He laughs. "You know you'd love to play principal. Admit it." He pokes me in the ribs.

"Okay, okay, I admit it. Sometimes I dream about playing principal. Just for a little while. Just to see what it's like to have the audience watching *me* for change, instead of Tawni. Just to see if it makes me play any better or feel differently about the music." I take a deep breath. "But that's one dream that will never come true as long as Tawni is in the orchestra. She is *so* good."

"So are you," says Colby seriously.

"Anyway," I say quickly, "Tawni should be here any minute. She's only missing the first half of practice because it's an important meet for her gymnastics team."

Colby wanders off to talk to one of the percussionists, a girl who goes to his school.

I pretend to study my music. But really I'm thinking about what Colby said. The more I think about it, the more I realize that I wouldn't mind being cello number one for a change. Just because Tawni has always played first doesn't mean she always *should* play first. Maybe I'll get a chance one day. Maybe at next year's auditions, I'll come out on top. Maybe...

"Five minutes, orchestra," Mr. Holmes calls.

Oh, who am I kidding? The reality is, no matter how hard I work, how much I practice, I will never be as good as Tawni. She lives inside the music in a way I can't. I don't know how she does it.

Mr. Holmes interrupts my daydream. "Brielle, Colby, I need a moment," he calls to us. He makes a beeline for the cello section, clutching his phone and frowning. Colby rushes over.

"I just heard from Tawni's mother," Mr. Holmes says. "Bad news. Tawni broke her wrist at her gymnastics event. She's not coming to rehearsal today."

I gasp. "Is she going to be okay? When will she be back?"

"That sucks," says Colby. "How bad is it?"

"It sounds like Tawni will be out of commission for at least three months," says Mr. Holmes. He's staring at me. I can see the wheels turning in his brain.

By this time the other cellists have gathered around to find out what's going on.

"We have to shift the cello section around," says Mr. Holmes firmly.

I am holding my breath.

"Congratulations, Brielle. You are now principal cellist."

Two

irst cellist? Me?

I gasp. "Mr. Holmes, I'm not—"

"We won't worry about switching seats right now," he interrupts. "Stay where you are for today. At our next rehearsal, Brielle will move to first chair. The rest of you will shift too. I'll let you know who will sit where."

This is happening too fast. I'm not ready for first chair. I don't want to be right in front of the audience during concerts. I don't want everyone looking at me.

"Mr. Holmes," I plead, "can't you find another principal cellist from another orchestra?"

He ignores me and bellows to the rest of the musicians, "Break's over, everyone." His voice fills the auditorium. "Please take your seats."

I'm practically hyperventilating.

This is all my fault. If only I hadn't wished to be first cello. If only I hadn't said it out loud, maybe Tawni would be okay. I jinxed my best friend. I should have kept my big mouth shut.

Colby slides over and punches my shoulder. "You rock, Brie! I told you that you were good enough to be principal cellist. And I am quite happy to move up to second chair, thank you very much."

He raises his hand to high-five me. I force a smile and slap his open palm. He turns and fist-bumps Jaron, who sits in the center of the back row of cellists.

Easy for Colby to be excited. He doesn't have to sit at the front of the orchestra. In full view of the audience. Right beside the conductor.

He has the best position now—my position. The second-chair cellist gets to play all the good lines in the music, but has no responsibility. No expectations. No spotlight.

"What's going on, Bum?"

I turn and glare at my brother, Marc. He plays double bass. That means he stands behind us cellists during practices and performances.

Sometimes during rehearsals he pokes me in the back with his bow. His mission in life is to bug me.

That includes calling me Bum. My initials are B.M. for Brielle Moran. Marc turned that into B-U-M when we were little. I hate it, and he knows it. That's why he still says it. Typical annoying big brother.

Right now, I'm not in the mood to be picked on.

"What did Mr. Holmes say to you?" asks my snoopy sibling.

I fill him in. "And don't call me Bum," I add.

"Sor-ree, Madame Cello Queen," he snips and picks up his double bass.

Mr. Holmes taps his baton on his music stand to get the group's attention.

"Before we continue with our rehearsal, I have some news," he announces. He tells everyone about Tawni's broken wrist and the soon-to-be-rearranged cello section. "Brielle is now our principal cellist."

A few people clap for me. Others murmur.

"Whaaat?"

"No way."

"Poor Tawni."

I focus on my bow, pretending to adjust the tension on the horsehair. I feel everyone staring at me. I know most of them think I'm not good enough to play first cello. I think they might be correct.

"It's too late in the season to find another musician," continues Mr. Holmes, "so we'll make do with five cellists for the rest of the year. We have a strong cello section, and I know Brielle will work with the others to make this a seamless transition."

Please, Mr. Holmes, don't put me in charge, screams the voice inside my head. *I don't want that responsibility. I don't want to be section leader.*

It's bad enough that as first cellist I have to sit front and center onstage. But it also means I'm the boss of the section. It's now my job to make sure the other cellists know what they're doing at all times.

I have to know all the cello parts inside and out. I have to make sure the others come in on the right beat. I have to correct them if they are playing too quickly or slowly, too softly or loudly. I have to be the go-between between the cellists and the conductor. If he has any problems with anything in the cello section, I have to fix it.

I don't want this job. I'm not ready. Pick someone else! Someone older.

Mr. Holmes is still talking. I keep my eyes on my bow, doing my best to keep breathing when all I feel like doing is running out of the auditorium.

I swipe a cake of sticky rosin over the bow. It needs just the right amount of rosin to create friction between the horsehair and the cello strings. The friction is what makes the sound.

I concentrate on that instead of looking at Mr. Holmes or the other musicians. I feel my face turning bright red. I don't want anyone to notice.

"Okay, that's enough about that," says Mr. Holmes.

Finally.

He rearranges the music on his stand. "Let's put *Marche Slave* away for now and work on something a little more upbeat for the rest of today's rehearsal," he says, flipping through the pages of a thick score.

I hear gossipy whispers from the viola section as the musicians pick up their instruments and reach for their music.

"Let's look at the last few lines of the Mozart piece, starting at..." Mr. Holmes is still scanning his music—and the viola section is still gossiping. "Starting at bar 179."

The "Mozart piece," as Mr. Holmes calls it, is *The Magic Flute Overture. The Magic Flute* is an opera. Wolfgang Amadeus Mozart wrote it more than two hundred years ago. The overture is the part of the opera that the orchestra plays right at the beginning, while the curtain is going up, before the singers start singing. It's six and a half minutes of lively, fun music.

Colby pokes me in the arm with his bow and flashes me a silly, cross-eyed grin. I flash him a don't-bug-me look, but he just laughs. Colby's goofiness almost makes me forget how stressed I am. I can't help but smile as I organize my sheet music.

I find bar 179 in the score, place my bow on the A string and position my fingers on the fingerboard. Mr. Holmes raises his baton and counts us in.

Three

On the drive home from rehearsal, Marc turns into this let-me-give-you-some-brotherly-advice guru guy.

"Listen, Bum..."

I shoot him a killer glare.

"Okay. Okay. *Brie-elle*," he says, rolling his eyes.

"Keep your eyes on the road, not in the sky," I scold. That just makes him roll his eyes again.

Marc just got his driver's license, so our parents let him have the van on rehearsal days. We need it to haul around his double bass and my cello, but I'm still nervous with him at the wheel.

"Listen to me, little sister," he says. "I've been principal bass for almost two years. It's no biggie. All the musicians know what they're doing.

If they weren't good players, they wouldn't be in the City Youth Orchestra."

"But you only have two double-bass players to worry about. I have four other cellists," I whine. "Plus, you're older than everyone in your section. They listen to you. I'm one of the youngest cellists. It's been hard enough for them to accept me in second chair, let alone as principal."

I heave a sigh and slump deep into the passenger seat. I love the feeling of bad posture after sitting at attention—back straight, elbows up, eyes front—for the past two hours in rehearsal.

I pull out my phone to text Tawni. **R U okay?**

"Look at the bright side," Marc continues. "The fact that you're now principal cellist means you're the best in the section. You'll get to play all the cello solos that come up."

Ack! I hadn't even thought of that. *That's the bright side?* This just gets worse and worse.

Marc is right. On top of being in charge of the whole cello section, *and* sitting center stage, now I'll have to play all by myself sometimes—with nobody between me and the audience.

"What if I screw up?" I cry.

My phone chirps. Tawni. **Not happy. Arm hurts.** 🙁

15

"Brie, don't be such a loser," Marc says. "Don't you get how great this is? You love playing cello. You're good at it. This is your chance to show everyone how good you are. Every other cellist in the orchestra would kill for this opportunity, and you're being a jerk about it."

Whatever.

I type. **R U at home?**

I remember when Marc was promoted to principal bass at the beginning of last year. He wasn't freaked out at all. He was totally amped when he got the news! He's always been so sure of himself. Unlike me.

Marc is sixteen now, so this is his last year in intermediate orchestra. Next fall he goes into twelfth grade. That means he has to audition for senior City Youth Orchestra this summer. He'll be competing with college and university students for one of four double-bass positions. Only the absolute best get in.

Marc is an excellent player, but he must be nervous—even though he'd never admit it. The tryouts are still four months away, but he's already chosen his audition pieces and started practicing.

Reply from Tawni. **In bed. Mom's orders.** ☹
I text right back. **Talk when I get home?**
K.

*   *   *

Hauling a cello around is a pain in the butt. It's
so big. But at least it's not a double bass. Marc's
instrument is taller than he is, and it weighs a
ton. I help him slide it out of the back of the van
when we get home. He lays it on its side in the
driveway, then helps me pull out the cello.

"Guess what?" he yells as soon as we enter
the house. "You now have *two* of the orchestra's
top musicians in the family!"

Mom greets us at the top of the stairs at the
side door. "That's no big news," she says, smiling.
"I've always known that."

Marc heads down the stairs to put his bass away
in our practice room. "Ask Bum what happened at
rehearsal today," he calls over his shoulder.

I follow him downstairs with my cello. Mom
tails me. Dad joins the parade.

"Well, Brielle?" Mom says. "Don't keep us in
suspense. What happened?"

"Tawni wasn't at rehearsal because she was at a gymnastics meet," I say. I carefully put my cello down beside my practice chair. "Then Mr. Holmes got a phone call from Tawni's mom. She said Tawni broke her wrist, so she won't be able to play cello for months."

Mom gasps.

"Aw, poor girl," says Dad.

Marc jumps in to hurry the story along. "And then Mr. Holmes announced to the whole orchestra that he's promoting Brie to principal cello."

Mom gasps again—in a happy way this time. "Brie, that's fantastic. I'm so proud of you!"

"That's great news, kiddo," says Dad. "You must be thrilled!"

"Ummm. I guess," I say. "But what if—"

"Oh, for Pete's sake," Marc interrupts. "Mr. Holmes just handed you an amazing opportunity. Deal with it."

He slams a pile of sheet music onto a stand. "The only person who has anything to gripe about right now is Tawni. You just took her job—and all you can do is whine about it. She'd trade places with you in a second if she could."

He stomps upstairs.

I take a deep breath. Marc is right about Tawni. I'm sure she's sick about all this.

"I know this is going to be tough on Tawni," says Mom. "But it's a wonderful opportunity for you, Brielle."

Dad chimes in. "We can't wait to see you sitting right at the front of the orchestra. We'll have to get that on video!"

Groan.

The family parade marches upstairs. Mom and Dad go into the kitchen, where Marc is stuffing his face with leftover spaghetti.

I turn down the hall toward my room. "I have to talk to Tawni, to make sure she's okay."

I fire up my computer. Tawni is already logged in and waiting for me. When I click on her profile picture, her face fills my screen. As soon as she sees me, tears start gushing from her eyes.

"I can't believe how stupid I am," she cries. "All I was doing was an easy turn-jump-cartwheel combination on the balance beam. I've done it a thousand times. But this time, I did the spin and the jump too fast." She pulls a tissue from a box beside her. She wipes her eyes and blows her nose. "When I went to do the cartwheel, my hand slipped off the beam. I went face first to the ground. Look what happened." She holds up her left arm to show me a cast. "I broke my wrist and my thumb."

"Does it still hurt?"

"A bit. They gave me pain pills at the hospital. I think they're starting to work." She sniffles and wipes her nose on her sleeve. "I got to ride in an ambulance though. That was kinda cool."

"An ambulance?" I say, surprised. "Your parents didn't drive you?"

"They weren't there."

"Seriously? They weren't at your gym meet? It was a really important—"

"Oh, they never go," says Tawni. "My dad was at some community meeting where everyone complains about everything. And Mom was at her squash club."

Weird. My parents never miss a single concert, track meet or spelling bee that Marc and I are in.

"They're actually a bit mad at me right now," Tawni says. "Meeting me at the hospital totally screwed things up for them today."

"That's ridiculous," I tell her. "They're not mad at you. They're upset that you got hurt."

Tawni looks down at her cast. She taps on it with the fingers of her right hand. "I hope so," she says quietly to her arm. When she looks up, she changes the subject. "Hey, I'm sorry I missed orchestra practice this aft. What happened after my mom phoned Holmes?"

I tell her about the conductor's announcement to the whole orchestra and how everyone was bummed about her injury.

"What's going to happen in the cello section?" Tawni asks with a little choke in her voice. "Are you taking my place?"

I feel terrible telling her this. She's in bed, in pain, with a broken wrist—and I've just been promoted because of it. "Just until you're better, Tawni. Of course, you'll play first cello again as soon as you're ready. It's still your chair. I'm just filling in."

"I will *never* do gymnastics again," Tawni vows. "It's not worth it. I'll die if I can't play cello anymore!"

She's being a drama queen right now. But I know she loves her cello more than anything.

That's what makes her so good. Her whole heart is in the music. She practices every chance she gets. Not because she has to, but because she *wants* to.

I like playing cello too, but I'm not obsessed with it the way Tawni is.

"You'll be back so soon that I won't even have time to get comfortable in your chair!" I say, trying to cheer her up.

Her eyes fill with tears again—we both know it's not true. She'll be out for months.

"Tawni, I don't *want* first chair. I don't *want* to be principal cellist. I'm not ready. I'm not you. You *have* to come back in time for the end-of-the-year concert!"

"Bee, if anyone is going to sit in my chair while I'm away, I want it to be you. I also want you to kick Colby's butt if he comes in too early in *Marche Slave*. He always does!"

She laughs and shakes her head, picturing Colby screwing up. "And watch Mr. Holmes's left hand. When he snaps his fingers, it means he's happy with how we're playing. Like he's secretly applauding us." She snaps with her right hand to show me, because her left is out of commission.

I've never noticed Mr. Holmes doing that.

"Another thing. Make sure you're the first one in your chair, ready to play, at every rehearsal."

Now that I think about it, I realize that Tawni was always seated, music ready, bow in hand, before the rest of us arrived.

"As principal cellist, I—I mean, *you* have to set a good example for the others."

I hadn't even thought about the role-model part of the job—one more thing to worry about.

"Bee, it's a real high being principal cellist," Tawni says, smiling sadly. "I love it. You will too, once you get used to it."

I hope she's right.

"I bet you'll love it so much that I'll have to arm-wrestle you to get my job back!"

I doubt that, but at least by the time we log off, we're both laughing and feeling better.

Four

practice like mad all week. I want to make sure that by the time I sit in that principal chair at next Sunday's rehearsal, I'm ready.

Tawni wants to make sure I'm ready too. Every time I see her, she gives me pointers.

"You should do finger exercises," she says after school on Monday as we walk to the bus stop.

Two years ago, Tawni moved to another part of town. She was supposed to transfer to a new school when her family moved. But our district has the best strings program, so she got permission to stay. It means, though, that she has to bus to school now.

It also means we don't walk home together the way we used to. Most days, I hang out with her at the bus stop while she waits for her ride.

"Finger exercises?" I say. "Seriously? That's a thing?"

"They'll make your hands stronger, so you'll be a better cellist," Tawni says. "There are tons of them. I do them every day." She holds up her right hand and clenches her fist. "Now I only do them with one hand. But I still do them." She shakes her hand out. "Do it with me," she says. "Close your hand as tight as you can."

I hold up one hand and make a fist.

"Now open your fingers as wide as you can." I copy her.

"No. Stretch your fingers even more. Like this." That looks painful.

"Now do it with both hands at the same time."

Good thing I'm wearing a knapsack, so both hands are free.

"You should do that five times a day," Tawni says. "Here's another one."

This time she has me bend my fingers at the first knuckle. "Now open and stretch. Good. Do it again."

I do it a couple more times.

"The best part is that you can do these exercises when you're sitting in class. Nobody will even notice." Tawni shakes out her right hand. "Now try this one."

She grabs her thumb inside her fist and straightens her arm in front of her. "Then you pull your thumb toward the ground and—"

Ouch. "I think that's enough for today, teach," I interrupt with a laugh. "My hand's starting to hurt."

* * *

On Tuesday Tawni and I eat lunch together. It's the only day of the week we have the same lunch period.

It's weird how little I see her these days. This semester, for the first time, we don't have a single class together. Our regular Tuesday lunch date is one of the only times Tawni and I see each other at school now. And because she won't be at orchestra practices anymore, I won't see her there either.

I scan the crowded cafeteria for Tawni. She's not here yet. I line up to buy a drink, then find space at one of the long tables. I save Tawni a seat.

"Tawni," I call when she comes in. "Over here."

She waves with her good hand and heads my way.

She pushes past other kids at the table to get to the chair across from me. "Hey, Bee, I had a brainwave this morning." She's talking before she even sits down.

I reach across the table to help my one-handed bestie get her lunch out of her knapsack.

"You need a practice schedule," she continues as she sits. "I made you one."

I unwrap her sandwich and open her juice box.

"I know you play your cello every day," she says. "But I thought a chart would help keep you organized."

"A chart?" I mumble through a mouthful of peanut-butter-and-jam sandwich.

She pulls a piece of paper out of the right-hand pocket of her jeans. "This lists all our orchestra pieces and which ones you should practice each day."

She pushes the paper across the table. "Here. Can you unfold it? I can't do it with one hand."

I open the page and smooth it out. I practically faint when I see Tawni's cramped writing. She has my whole life planned out!

"I make a schedule like this every semester."
Tawni is so excited she's practically bouncing in
her chair. "I thought it would be good for you to
have one now that...well, now that you're me."

I take a gulp from my carton of chocolate
milk. *Now that I'm you?*

"Look." She points to today's date—Tuesday,
February 28—on the diagram. "This afternoon
you start with *Marche Slave*. It's the one you
know best, so it'll give you confidence."

I study Tawni's schedule. My schedule. *It's
too much.*

"Tuesday, *Marche Slave*. Wednesday, *Magic
Flute*," I read out loud. "Thursday, exercises. Does
that mean I stretch my fingers some more?"

"Nooo," Tawni answers as if I'm completely clue-
less. "It means you should take a break from practicing the performance pieces at least once a week."

Yay. I get a day off!

"That doesn't mean you get a day off," she
says, as if I'd said it out loud. *Weird.* "You still
have to work hard that day, Bee."

I pull a banana out of my lunch bag. *Stop
telling me what to do*, I say in my head, hoping
she'll get that message too.

"That's the day you do things like running scales up and down all four strings," Tawni continues, obviously *not* reading my mind. "And focus on your finger placement on the fingerboard. You can work on bow strokes and pizzicato without thinking about it too much. I find it really helps me to..."

I tune her out. I know Tawni is trying to help, but she's freaking me out with her schedules and exercises and finger gymnastics.

"Tawni, I'm not you," I blurt out.

She freezes, her mouth open, poised to take a bite of her sandwich.

Neither of us speaks for a few seconds. She carefully places her sandwich on top of the baggie it came in. She looks down at her arm, rubs the cast. It has a few signatures and silly drawings on it already.

Instantly I feel terrible that I snapped at her. I know she's just trying to make me a better cellist—a principal cellist.

"What I mean," I say more kindly, "is that this is all new to me. You've been doing it for years."

"Which is exactly why I'm trying to help you," she says sharply. "You said you were scared about playing principal cello. And since I can't play right now, I thought I could help you instead. But if you don't care..."

She pulls a pouty face—like she always does when things don't go her way. It bugs me.

"It's not that I don't care," I say. "It's just too intense. I've only been principal cellist for two days, and it's already making my brain hurt." I grab my head with both hands and cross my eyes to prove it.

Tawni giggles. And stops pouting.

"I'm practicing a lot this week," I say. "But I don't want my whole life to be about cello."

Tawni takes a deep breath in and lets it out slowly. "Brielle," she says, as if she's my mother, "I know what I'm talking about."

Meaning I don't?

"If you're going to be principal cellist," she says, all teacher-like, "you have to take it more seriously. It's different than just *playing* in the orchestra. It's a big responsibility."

"Which is why I never wanted to do it in the first place," I whine.

"Well, I don't want you to have my job either," Tawni cries. "I'd give anything to be able to play right now."

I bite my lip. That's exactly what Marc said on Sunday. "*Tawni would give anything to trade places with you right now. And all you can do is whine about it.*"

I drink the last of my chocolate milk. Tawni picks at the crust of her sandwich. The pouty face has returned.

I know I should be grateful for the chance to play principal cello. And I know I should listen to Tawni—she's one of the best cellists in the city. But does she have to be so bossy about everything?

"I can't play cello right now," Tawni says quietly. "I can't do gymnastics. I can't do much of anything."

Her pout has turned into a full-on sulk.

"All I can do is sit at home and listen to my parents nag me."

"Why are they nagging?"

"It doesn't matter. I thought if I could help you, it would give me something to do. And get me out of the house."

She starts packing up her leftover lunch. I reach across the table to give her a helping hand—since she only has one good one now.

It must be a drag being one-handed and not able to do the things you love to do. Tawni's used to being in charge of a cello section, and now she can't even play.

I don't want her taking over my life. But I don't want her to feel left out of everything either. She is my BFF, after all. And she really *is* trying to help me.

"Your idea about *Marche Slave* is good," I admit. "You're right. It *will* give me confidence. I'll work on it after school today."

She perks up. "Do you want me to come over and help you?"

Whoa, sister! Practicing side by side at orchestra rehearsals *with* Tawni is one thing. Having her stare over my shoulder while I'm playing by myself would totally stress me out.

"I'm good with *Marche Slave*," I say. "Maybe you could help me another day, when I'm working on one of the harder pieces."

"Okay, how about tomorrow when you work on the Mozart?"

"How about we just go back to class right now and worry about Mozart later?" I hold my head and cross my eyes again. "Remember what I said about my brain hurting?"

"Yeah, yeah." She laughs. "Let's go."

* * *

On Wednesday afternoon I run into Tawni between classes. Taylor Swift's "Shake It Off " is on my iPod. I'm doing a little dance-walk down the hallway. The song is a few years old, but I still love it. I can't help but move when I hear it.

Tawni interrupts my tunes—and my dancing mood. "I hope you're listening to recordings of our orchestra music," she says when we meet.

"Definitely," I lie, and pull out my earbuds.

"I have some good ones," she says. "I'll send them to you tonight."

"Okay," I say. "What class do you have now? I have French, but I have to stop at my locker before I go. So...see you later." I plug my earbuds back into my ears and turn to go.

"Bee, wait."

I twirl around to face her again. "What's up?" My finger is poised to press Play on my iPod.

"I forgot that I have a doctor's appointment after school," she says. "I won't be able to help you with the Mozart piece today after all."

"No worries," I say. "Another time."

What a relief! I like Tawni and everything, but I *really* don't want her breathing down my neck when I practice.

"Tomorrow is your day to do exercises instead of practicing," Tawni says, remembering the schedule she created for me. "Maybe Friday?"

"I'll text you," I say as I rush off.

Tawni's voice follows me down the hall. "You only have four days to get ready for your first rehearsal as principal!"

I turn and wave and press *Play*.

*   *   *

By the end of the week, Tawni is getting full-on annoying. It's nice that she wants to help, but her cello obsession is driving me crazy. She texted me nine times on Thursday. Then, when I waited for the bus with her after school, she made me practice finger exercises with her.

Today is Friday, and so far I've managed to avoid her. I need a break from her tips and suggestions, her recordings and her bossiness.

I know she misses her music, but it's all-cello-all-the-time with her. Too much for me.

Practice tonight? she texts. That's message number six for the day. I've only replied to three of them so far—but I can't keep ignoring her. I'm heading into my last class of the day.

Tawni, gimme a break! That's what I want to text to her. Instead, I write that Marc and I are going to practice together tonight. Which is sort of true. We're going to work on our music for an hour or so after school. But after dinner I have no intention of playing my cello.

My plan is to binge-watch old episodes of *The Vampire Diaries*. My parents wouldn't let me watch the show when it first came out, so I'm catching up on all the past episodes now that I'm allowed. I can't wait to veg out and forget about cello for a change.

Five

Come Sunday afternoon, Marc and I pile ourselves, our instruments and our music into the van. "You ready for your big debut, Bum-Bum?"

"If you call me Bum-Bum, or even a single Bum, during rehearsal, I will kill you." That came out sounding more confident than I feel.

In fact, I'm quite anxious about today's rehearsal, but I can't tell Marc that. I don't want to give my doofus of a brother any more ammo to use against me.

"I've practiced more this week than I've practiced in the last six months total," I say coolly. "I am good to go, bro."

My phone chirps. Tawni. **Break a leg this aft** ☺

I bet she's extra bummed now that it's orchestra day and she can't play.

Thx, I type, then shut off my phone.

I take Tawni's advice and make sure I'm the first cellist seated in the section. I have my bow rosined, my strings tuned and my music organized before any of the others arrive. Very role model-ish.

I look to my left, to where the audience would be sitting if this were a concert. There is nothing between me and the "house," as it's called. I am so close to the edge of the stage that I worry about falling off. I wonder whether any principal cellists have ever tumbled into the audience during a performance.

"Look at you, Ms. Cellist-in-Charge!"

I almost spring out of my chair.

"A little jumpy, are we?" Colby laughs. "Be careful you don't flip right off the stage."

"Ha, ha, ha. Very funny." That's the best reply I can come up with.

"Don't be nervous, Brie. Get over it."

"I didn't hear you coming, you sneak. That's all."

Mr. Holmes is heading our way. A man on a mission.

"Brielle. This is how I want the cello section to look in Tawni's absence."

He hands me a piece of paper with a diagram on it. It's a layout of the orchestra, showing five cello chairs instead of the usual six—three in the front row, two behind. Each chair is indicated by a square, and each square has a cellist's name on it.

"When the other cellists arrive, please organize them according to this chart," he says.

I study the drawing. I had assumed all of us would simply be promoted by one place. I was second cello, now I'm first. Colby was third, now he's second. And so on.

But I notice on the diagram that Ella, the sixth cellist, has been promoted to fourth, jumping ahead of Jaron.

"Mr. Holmes, I think there's a mistake on this. Shouldn't Jaron be fourth and Ella fifth?"

"Promotions are not automatic, Brielle," he says. "Please inform the others of their places in our new section."

I stop him as he turns to leave. "Mr. Holmes, I can't tell Jaron that he's not being promoted. He'll hate me."

"You're section leader now, Brielle. It's your job."

"But—"

Colby elbows me in the ribs, warning me to be quiet. Mr. Holmes heads back to his office.

"I'd be happy to take first chair if it's too much for you, Brie," Colby says sweetly. "I'd have no trouble telling that moron he's not being promoted."

On cue, Jaron arrives onstage, lugging his cello and pushing his way toward us. He goes to sit in the front chair of the second row—the fourth cellist's seat.

Colby nods his head toward Jaron. "Go pass on the good news," he whispers with glee.

I hate this.

"Hi, Jaron," I say. "Umm, Mr. Holmes made a chart showing how he wants the cello section arranged."

I show him the paper and point to his name in the fifth cellist's chair. "I'm sorry, but you are not being promoted right now," I say as nicely as I can.

"What are you talking about? Now that Tawni is out of the picture, everyone else gets to move up a place."

"I thought so too, but Mr. Holmes wants it this way." I point to the paper to prove it. "He said you are to stay in fifth position, and Ella will move to fourth."

"That is not fair, Brielle. Go talk to Holmes. I want to be fourth cellist." He plunks himself in fourth chair.

"Jaron, come on. You have to move. Ella's here."

He looks away, refusing to budge.

"Hi, everyone," Ella chirps. She's always so sweet. "What's going on?"

I explain that she is now fourth cellist and that Jaron is in her seat.

"Oh, I'm happy to play fifth and let Jaron move up," she says.

"See?" says Jaron.

"If it were up to me, that's how I would organize the section," I say, my voice shaking. "But it's not up to me. This is how Mr. Holmes wants it." I thrust the paper diagram in Ella's face.

Ella starts unpacking her cello. Jaron isn't moving. I don't know what to do.

"Dude, don't be a jerk. Move your butt to fifth chair." Marc has been watching from behind us in the bass section. Now he's looming over Jaron, double bass in hand.

"Oh, sure. Big brother to the rescue," Jaron sneers. "Doing baby sister's dirty work."

"Jaron, that's not fair," I say.

"Don't talk to me about fair, you little diva. What's not fair is that everyone is moving up in the section except me."

By now other musicians are watching the drama unfolding in the cello section.

Mr. Holmes is going to come out of his office any second and see that I don't have everyone ready to play, that I'm not in control of my section.

In one last effort to take charge, I put on the most commanding voice I can muster. "Jaron. Please. Switch. Seats. Now."

Four heads snap my way. Jaron, Marc, Colby and Ella are as surprised by my tone as I am.

"Jaron, please move, just for today," Ella pleads quietly. "We can sort this out for next week."

He shakes his head in disgust, stands up and moves one chair to the right. Glaring at me. "Just because you're now principal cellist, it doesn't mean you get to dump on the rest of us," he spits out.

"Thank you for giving Ella her seat," I say as calmly as I can before returning to my chair—just in time for Mr. Holmes to make his appearance.

My hands are shaking as I pick up my cello and bow and get ready to play.

*　　*　　*

It turns out that the scene with Jaron is just the beginning. The whole rehearsal is one disaster after another.

During *Marche Slave*, when I switch from pizzicato to bowing, I lose control of my bow. It flings out of my hand, bounces off the music stand with a clatter and lands at Mr. Holmes's feet. Colby, who now shares a music stand with me, muffles a laugh. I feel like an idiot.

I can't reach the bow on the floor without putting my cello down, getting out of my chair and crawling under the conductor's podium. So I have to sit there like a loser, not playing, until Mr. Holmes pauses rehearsal to ask us to replay a section.

Later, in *The Magic Flute Overture*, my eyes jump ahead a line, and I play a whole series of wrong notes before I can stop myself. Mr. Holmes cringes and scowls at me.

At the beginning of our break, I put my cello down and stand up to stretch. Marc reaches between Ella and Jaron to poke me in the back with his bow. I freak out and spin around to yell at him. My bow, still in my hand, whacks Colby in the head. He falls backward in his chair, knocking over Ella and Jaron's music stand on the way down. Jaron jumps out of the way just in time, but the stand crash-lands on his cello. Sheet music goes flying.

I am frozen in place, watching this nightmare play out, my mouth open like a fish gasping for air.

When the dust settles, the room is deadly quiet. Every eye in the orchestra is focused on the cello section. I hear a few sniggers. Then the whispers begin.

Ella starts gathering scattered sheet music. Marc, looking sheepish, mouths *Sorry* to me. Colby, of course, is lying on the floor, laughing his head off.

"Great job, O mighty leader," sneers Jaron. "I can't believe anyone would put you in charge. If my cello is damaged, you are going to pay for it, you loser."

Don't cry. Don't cry. Don't cry, I tell myself.

Colby picks himself up. "That was awesome, Brie! I hope someone caught it on video!"

Marc makes his way to us. "Bum—" he begins.

"Leave me alone," I snap, holding back tears.

He and Colby exit the rehearsal area, collecting a group of high-fiving, hand-shaking buddies as they head to the break room. They're all howling.

Yeah, guys, I'm a riot.

I plunk myself into Colby's chair, second chair, *my* chair. I pull out my phone to text Tawni. I wish she were here. I wish everything would go back to normal.

We miss u, I type.

☹ **Wish I was there** ☹ is her quick reply.

I don't know what else to say, so I put my phone away. I spend the entire break sitting in the second cellist's chair. I feel like hiding under it.

Fifteen minutes later, our break is over. I move back to first chair, and all the other musicians in the orchestra take their seats. Some of them smile sympathetically in my direction. Others are still smirking.

"Ready for round two?" Colby asks as he sits down.

Fortunately, round two, the second half of rehearsal, is uneventful. I don't play particularly well, but at least I don't do anything stupid or clumsy.

"Good work today, everyone," Mr. Holmes says as we finish up. "And thank you to the cello section for entertaining us this afternoon!"

The whole orchestra cracks up. A wave of heat washes over my face.

It's bad enough that I made such a mess of everything today. Did he have to remind everybody?

"At our next rehearsal, we're going to focus on *Capriccio Espagnol*," he says. "Practice well this week." He faces me and continues. "As you all know, *Capriccio Espagnol* has a lovely cello part in it—which means that our new principal cellist will be playing her first solo for us!"

Six

I can't believe I have to perform the solo in *Capriccio Espagnol* already. It's only my second week as principal cellist!

You'd think Mr. Holmes would cut me some slack—especially after that last disastrous rehearsal. I'm surprised he even wants to keep me on as principal after the mess I made of everything.

"Bee, it's only thirteen bars," says Tawni when I tell her about the solo. She's played it many times. "It's not hard. You're just stressed because you've never played by yourself before."

It's true. Tawni and I have played duets together in the past. I was okay with that because there were two of us. But a solo is a whole different ball game. A terrifying ball game.

"How do you get to Carnegie Hall?" Tawni asks me. It's a stupid riddle we've heard a hundred times. I don't give her the punch line she's looking for.

"Well, first you fly to New York City, then you get on the subway—"

"Har har. Very funny, Bee. How do you get to Carnegie Hall?"

"Practice, practice, practice," we recite together, laughing at the lame old joke.

"Yeah yeah," I say. "I get it."

*   *   *

I run through *Capriccio Espagnol* over and over again all week. *Capriccio Espagnol* is a set of five songs based on Spanish folk music. Weirdly, though, it wasn't written by a Spanish composer. A Russian guy named Nikolai Rimsky-Korsakov wrote *Capriccio Espagnol* in 1887. My solo comes about halfway through the fourth song, a four-minute tune called "Gypsy Song."

My goal is to learn the music inside and out. When I'm not practicing, I'm studying the score.

I carry the sheet music with me everywhere, in case I get a spare minute to review it.

Sometimes, when I'm riding in the car or sitting at the breakfast table, I pretend I'm holding my cello. Like air guitar, only it's air cello. I go through the motions, using my shoulder as a stand-in for the fingerboard and a pencil or a knife for a bow.

In bed at night, I visualize my fingers making the notes. I see the bow strokes in my mind.

I practice, and I memorize—and by rehearsal day, I feel good about it.

Just to be sure I'm ready, though, I do something I hate doing.

I find Marc in the kitchen. Eating, as usual. It's eleven o'clock, and he's finally up, having breakfast.

"Marc, do you think you could tear yourself away from that bacon to help me with *Capriccio Espagnol*?"

"Ha! I knew you'd come running to me eventually," he says, painting a piece of toast with strawberry jam. "It's nice to know you need me, little sister."

"I don't need *you*. I need your double bass."

"Well, you know where it is. Downstairs in the practice room."

"You know what I mean. I want to practice one more time, and it would be good to hear the cello and bass together."

"Meaning you *need* me," he says.

Marc is such a jerk sometimes. "Yes, Marc," I say. "I need you."

"Well, ask politely, and I might consider it."

"Seriously? Can't you be nice to me for once? Forget it. I'll practice on my own." I storm downstairs.

Marc follows, toast in hand. "Geez, Bum, don't get so out of whack about it. I'm just giving you a hard time. It's my brotherly duty."

I ignore him and rosin my bow.

"If you give me half a second to wash the jam off my hands, I'll play with you," he says. "I could use the warm-up before today's rehearsal anyway."

I run scales to loosen my fingers while I'm waiting for him.

It takes Marc forever to wash his hands, unpack his bass, rosin his bow, tune his strings, prep his music and do a quick warm-up.

"Okay, let's do this!" he says finally.

We spend the next hour running through three different numbers, including *Capriccio Espagnol*. I play my solo perfectly, if I do say so myself!

"Little sister, I am impressed," Marc says when we're done. "It sounds like you actually know how to play that thing. Even your solo was good—for a beginner."

I give him a dirty look. That's the closest thing to a compliment I'll ever get out of my brother. He always has to get a dig in.

"Let's call it a wrap," he says. "I'm done. People to see, places to go. You know how it is."

"I'm going to stay and practice a bit more."

"Bum, you'll psyche yourself out if you overdo it. You're ready. Take a break before rehearsal."

I suppose he's right. That was a good run-through. I should quit while I'm ahead.

"Kid, you're a good cellist. You deserve to play principal."

Did I just hear a full-on compliment come out of Marc's mouth?

"And Bum?" He pauses. "If you tell anyone I said that, I'll have to kill you!"

* * *

At this afternoon's rehearsal, we spend most of our time working on *Capriccio Espagnol.* My solo comes near the end of the piece, so we don't get to it until after our break.

"Let's pick up where we left off," says Mr. Holmes at the start of the second half of rehearsal. "We'll start at letter *N,* just after the harp solo."

I take a deep breath my solo starts ten bars after letter *N.*

I know I can do this. Marc even said so.

Mr. Holmes raises his baton, and off we go.

The ten bars leading into my solo are all the same. Pizzicato. Low A for two counts. Rest for one. High A for two counts. Rest for one.

Four bars until my solo. Three. Two. One.

I take a breath. Mr. Holmes gives me my cue.

The orchestra goes quiet.

C, B-flat, C, B-flat, A, B-flat, A, B-flat, A. Short rest.

So far so good.

1-2-3, 4-5-6. F, G, F, E, F, E...

I know this by heart, so I barely have to think. I've played these thirteen bars so many times, they almost play themselves.

I focus on my fingers. I count in my head. I play each note perfectly!

Twenty seconds later, it's over. The rest of the orchestra comes back in.

I did it! I played my first solo!

I can't stop to pat myself on the back, because the piece isn't over yet. But I'm feeling pretty pumped about it. I can breathe again.

Four minutes later we reach the end of the number. The last fifteen bars are loud. They're fast. Every instrument is playing. Then, with three final, dramatic notes, *Capriccio Espagnol* is over.

Mr. Holmes puts down his baton. "Thank you, orchestra," he says. "Nice work."

I'm beaming. I know he means me. I'm feeling pretty proud of myself. Maybe I am meant to be principal cellist after all!

"Brie, you did great!" Colby taps me on the head with his bow.

Mr. Holmes looks at me and gives me a little bow. "Congratulations, Brielle. You just played your first solo. Good work!"

The other musicians clap or tap their bows on their music stands. The drummer plays a little drum roll. Marc reaches between the cellists behind me to poke me with his bow.

"All right, everyone, let's move on," Mr. Holmes says to the group. "Time to put aside *Capriccio Espagnol* and have some fun. Let's do...'Bad Romance.'"

"Yes!" says Ella behind me. We all love playing this Lady Gaga tune, but it's Ella's favorite. She's such a huge Gaga fan, she can't help but sing along.

Now that I'm principal cellist, I suppose it's my job to tell her not to. But I'm on a bit of a high right now, so I'm going to let her have some fun with it.

The trombones open with the familiar line.

"*Rah rah ah-ah-ah! Ro mah ro-mah-mah! Ga-ga ooh-la-la!*" Ella thinks she's singing softly, but we can all hear her. Mr. Holmes gives her a fake glare, but even he has to laugh.

It's a three-minute piece, so we do it a couple of times before he dismisses us for the day. "Thanks, everyone. Nice job this afternoon."

I loosen the horsehair on my bow and put the bow on the music stand. A few of the other musicians come over to congratulate me on my first solo. I take my time packing up.

Mr. Holmes makes his way through the chairs to the trumpet section to give the players some feedback. Everyone knows they played too loudly in the final song of *Capriccio Espagnol.* Totally drowned out the clarinets and flutes.

I pull out my phone to text Tawni. **Played solo! H said it was good!** ☺

"I'll meet you outside," Marc says as he rushes past. "I want to grab Paul before he takes off." Paul is principal violinist, one of Marc's best friends.

Mr. Holmes is moving through the orchestra, section by section, giving notes to various musicians. Eventually, he heads my way.

"Brielle," he says, beckoning me away from the other cellists. "You've obviously practiced your solo."

I nod and smile. "I worked really hard this week." I sense he's about to praise me for my brilliant performance this afternoon.

"It wasn't bad," he continues. "You got all the notes in all the right places."

Wasn't bad? Notes in the right places? That doesn't sound like praise.

"Now I need you to work on smoothing it out. I want you to *feel* the music. Anyone with a cello can play the notes, but I want you to *make music.*"

Thank goodness we're far enough away from the others that they can't hear this. Jaron would have a field day.

"Oh, okay. Yes, sir. I'll work on that."

Mr. Holmes leaves me and heads toward the viola section. I return to my chair to finish packing up my instrument and music.

My phone beeps with a reply from Tawni. **Told you it was easy!** ☺

Talk about bad timing.

I shut off the phone without texting back.

My lower lip starts to quiver. I bite on it as I put my cello in its case.

"What did Holmes say?" Colby asks.

I can't help it. I start bawling. "He said I sucked! I knew I couldn't do this. I knew I wasn't good enough. I should just quit. I wish Tawni would come back."

I run outside to find Marc. I need to get away from Colby and Mr. Holmes and everything to do with music.

Seven

I haven't picked up my cello since Mr. Holmes told me he hated my solo. Maybe now he'll get someone else to play principal. Colby would love the top job—and he'd be better at it than I am.

"Hey, Crumb-Bum." Marc interrupts my crabby mood. "Watching TV again?"

"I happen to love *Bugs Bunny*," I snap. "So what?"

"Why don't you come downstairs and practice with me?" he says. "I'm going to work on *Magic Flute Overture*. It would be great to hear the bass and cello together."

"Not interested."

"Come on, you haven't practiced for days. Three days, to be exact. That's not like you."

"I said no. I want to watch this show."

Marc stands in front of the TV.

"Get lost," I yell.

"Brielle, you've been watching after-school cartoons all week instead of practicing." He grabs the remote and shuts off the TV. "What is up with you?"

"What's up with me? What's up with you?" I try to snatch the remote from his hand. He pulls it out of my reach.

"Whatever," I say. "Leave me alone."

I pick up a magazine from the coffee table and pretend to read it.

"Since when do you read *Popular Woodworking*?" Marc says, stifling a laugh.

I give him the silent treatment.

"Brie, you have to practice," he says. "You are now principal cellist. That means you have to know the music better than anyone. You can't take a day off, let alone three. You have to—"

"Shut up, Marc. I don't *have* to do anything. I can't. I'm not good enough. Mr. Holmes said so."

"That's not at all what he said. He said your solo was good. And it can be even better. That's why we *rehearse*, little sister. To get better."

I ignore him.

"It's called *practice*, not *perfection*."

I can't help but snicker at my stupid brother being all, well, brotherly.

"Listen, if you weren't up to it, Holmes would never have put you in first chair. You've played second to Tawni since you were nine years old. Now you have a chance to be first, to prove you're as good as she is."

Marc is being super intense, like he actually cares about me and my music career.

He puts his hands on his hips, looks down at me on the couch and puts on his most grown-up voice. "And what are you doing with this opportunity, young lady? You're sitting on your butt, watching *Bugs Bunny*."

"Who are you, my dad?" I giggle. "You're such a goofball."

"Bum, I may never be this nice to you again. Don't blow it."

I stick out my tongue at him.

"Practice makes perfect and all that," Marc says. "So come on, let's go practice."

"Okay, okay, if you need my help that badly, I won't make you beg." I laugh and follow him downstairs.

*   *   *

For the next three weeks, Marc and I practice together a lot. I run through the music every day on my own too. It's amazing what a difference twenty-one days can make!

I'm getting to know the music so well that I am starting to feel the tones and rhythms in a whole new way. I used to see the notes as something to control, or to master. Now I find myself floating away with the music instead of fighting with it. I'm starting to understand Tawni's passion for playing.

Like Tawni, I'm now practicing because I *want* to. It has become my favorite thing to do.

Despite my rocky start as principal, I now look forward to weekly orchestra rehearsals. I love hearing my cello blending with all the other instruments, creating harmonies and musical images.

Colby, Grant and Ella have accepted me as principal—now that I have begun to accept myself in the position. I've been getting great feedback from them on my playing. They've started coming to me for advice, the way we all used to go to Tawni.

Last week Grant asked me to help him with a section of *Marche Slave*. It's the piece I know best, so I was happy to work with him. And a few days ago Colby asked me to meet him for an extra rehearsal. Now that he's second cello, he has new lines of music to learn. We practiced together for about two hours—until he felt good about the new passages.

"I don't know what you've been doing lately, Brie, but your playing is amazing," he said as we packed up. "You've always been good, but now you're better than Tawni ever was."

"I don't think that is true." I blushed. "But... ummm...thanks."

Helping Colby and Ella and Grant has made me realize that I actually *do* know what I'm doing. Coaching them has become my favorite part of my new job.

I'm beginning to believe I might be cut out for playing principal cello after all.

*   *   *

Tawni's been weird lately. We still meet for lunch on Tuesdays, but otherwise I hardly see her. And when I do, she's a bit of a drag. She doesn't want to talk about orchestra. Or cello. Or practicing. Or anything related to music. She doesn't even try to butt in on my practices anymore

Today, though, I just can't help talking about it. "I have to tell you about Sunday's rehearsal," I say as soon as we're sitting down. "It was amazing. The cello section kicked butt! Even Jaron played well for once."

As always, I help her unpack her knapsack and her lunch. It's been a month since Tawni broke her wrist and thumb. She's getting better at doing everything one-handed. But I still want to be there for her.

"You were right, Tawni," I continue. "It's a total high being principal cellist—especially when we have such a perfect rehearsal!"

"So my practice schedule has been useful?" she asks. "I told you it would help."

Shoot. I haven't been using her stupid chart.

"Well, actually, I've sort of come up with my own way to learn the music," I confess. "Marc and I—"

"Marc isn't a cellist," Tawni interrupts.

"I know, but we work well together. He's been a section leader for almost two years."

"And I've been a section leader for forever, Bee." Here comes the pouty face. "I know what I'm talking about."

I stuff a spoonful of yogurt into my mouth, because I don't know what to say.

I know Tawni's choked that I'm not using her lame-o schedule. But I'm choked right back at her. The more confidence I'm gaining as first cellist, the more moody she's getting. She's totally bumming me out these days.

"It's not the same at rehearsals without you," I say, trying to cheer her up. "I hope you'll be back soon. How's the arm?"

"Still in a cast."

Ouch. Chilly—and pouty.

I finish my yogurt and pull a cookie out of my lunch bag.

I do the only thing I can think of doing. "Hey, how did you do on your math test yesterday?" I change the subject.

* * *

"Brielle, could you show me the proper bowing for this passage?" Ella approaches me before the start of Sunday's rehearsal. "I don't think I'm doing it right."

I demonstrate the correct bowing. Ella pencils some notes in her score so she'll remember the moves.

Ella's learning curve since being promoted from sixth to fourth cellist has been huge—almost as huge as mine. She's had to learn lots of new lines of music, and she's had to cope with Jaron's griping. Her hard work is paying off. Her playing has improved amazingly. I can see why Mr. Holmes promoted her past Jaron.

Meanwhile, Jaron's performance hasn't improved at all. In fact, it seems to have gotten worse. I'm constantly correcting him and passing on feedback to him from Mr. Holmes. I hate doing it, because Jaron is a total jerk whenever I speak to him. It's the part of the job I like the least.

I wonder if Jaron was like this with Tawni or if he's acting like this because he's still choked about not moving up in the section.

Tap, tap, tap. Mr. Holmes raps his baton on his music stand to get our attention.

"Good afternoon, everyone," he bellows over the bustle of musicians chatting, shuffling pages of music and moving their chairs into position. "Take your seats, please." He waits for quiet.

I look around to make sure the cello section is ready. Other than Jaron, who is texting, we are all focused on the conductor. "Jaron," I whisper sharply. He ignores me.

"As you know," says Mr. Holmes, "our Family and Friends concert is only three weeks away. I'd like to run through our entire repertoire today to see which pieces need work and which ones are in good shape."

He picks up a score from the stack of music on the table by his side. He places it on his music stand and opens it to the first page. "Let's start with *Capriccio Espagnol*," he says. "It's been weeks since we've looked at it."

Noooo, I wail in my head. *Can't we warm up with other pieces first?*

"Hey, Brie, you get to play your solo again!" Colby whispers. He shuffles through our music until he finds the right pages. "You're going to rock it this time!"

I feel sick when I remember my last experience with this piece. Mr. Holmes hated how I played it three weeks ago.

I feel a gentle poke in my back. I turn around to glare at Marc. For once, though, he's not poking me with his bow to bug me. He's giving me a smile and two thumbs up. "You've got this," he says just loudly enough for me to hear.

"I doubt it," says Jaron.

Mr. Holmes glances toward the cello section, then raises his baton to count us in.

I can do this, I tell myself. *I've practiced my solo a hundred times since that first try.*

Mr. Holmes has us play the whole piece from start to finish. It's a long composition—about sixteen minutes. My solo is at the eleven-minute mark. I play it. The rest of the orchestra comes back in, and we finish the piece.

As the final notes ring through the auditorium, Mr. Holmes puts down his baton. He writes something in his music. He doesn't say a word.

I bite my lip. Colby punches me in the shoulder. "That was great," he whispers. I hope he's right. I think I played the solo well—but that's what I thought the last time too.

Finally, Mr. Holmes puts down his pencil and lifts his eyes. He turns my way. I pretend to tune one of my strings instead of meeting his gaze.

"Brielle," he says in his booming voice.

I look up at him. "Yes, sir?"

"Brielle, you have obviously practiced your solo in the last few weeks. You got all the notes in the right places, just like last time."

Oh no, not again. I nod my head, but I feel like throwing up.

"This time, though, you made it sing! That was beautiful!"

Eight

Three weeks later, my whole family is sitting in the front row of the auditorium. Dad is already fussing with the video camera. Even if I play well today, there's a good chance I'll die of embarrassment.

Before any of them see me, I duck back into the music room.

It's two months before our major end-of-year performance. This afternoon's Family and Friends concert is a test run.

I tell myself it's just another practice. It's on our regular rehearsal day in our regular auditorium. No biggie.

The difference is that we're all dressed up. White tops. Black pants or skirts. Some of the girls are wearing makeup. The boys have combed their hair.

The other difference is that there are about 150 people in the house waiting to watch us play.

"This is your chance to perform for friendly faces," says Mr. Holmes at our pre-show pep talk in the music room. "Everyone in the audience today wants you to do well. No need to be nervous."

Easy for him to say. He's not performing as principal cellist for the first time. He's not playing a solo in front of all those people. *I hope I don't blow it.*

Usually nobody is allowed in the music room before a concert except the performers. This time, though, Mr. Holmes has admitted one visitor—Tawni.

After Mr. Holmes finishes boosting our team spirit, she makes her way to me and Colby.

"Hey, Tawni," Colby says. He hugs her. "How's the arm?"

"Still in a cast," she replies, holding it up to show him. "Which reminds me. You haven't signed it yet!"

He leaves us in search of a marker.

"I brought you something." Tawni places a little yellow box in my hand. "It's for good luck today."

"You didn't have to do that," I say. Suddenly I feel terrible for not spending any time with her lately.

I open the box and find a silver ring decorated with tiny music notes.

"I know we're not allowed to wear dangly jewelry when we play," says Tawni, "but I think you can get away with a pinkie ring."

I put the ring on the baby finger of my right hand. "It's perfect, Tawni. Thank you." I hug her.

"I'm sorry I've been so crabby lately. It's just that..." She's on the verge of tears. "I just wish I was playing with you this aft."

"Break it up. Break it up." Colby butts in and grabs Tawni's left hand. "I have a cast to sign." Things never get too serious with him around.

Colby manages to draw a bass clef and a pair of music notes on her cast before Mr. Holmes raps his baton on the nearest music stand.

"Showtime, everyone!" He waves his hand toward the door. "Tawni, thank you for your moral support. We'll see you after the concert."

"Break a leg, not a wrist," Tawni calls to the orchestra members as she heads out. I know she doesn't feel as cheery as she's pretending to be. I know she feels left out. This is the first concert she's missed in years.

"The rest of you, pick up your instruments and line up," Mr. Holmes orders.

We organize ourselves in the order we are to walk onto the stage. That means Marc is the first one to go, followed by the other two bass players. I'm next in line, with four cellists behind me. The rest of the musicians take their places for the march onstage.

The audience claps as we enter the auditorium and go to our seats.

I'm horrified to see that Dad is already recording. *Geez, Dad, we're just walking in. At least wait until something happens.*

We remain standing until all the musicians have reached their places. Together we take our seats. Our sheet music is already on our stands in the order we are to perform it.

After I'm settled, I sneak a peek over my left shoulder, toward the audience. My family is right under my nose. Dad's getting a nice shot up my nostrils. Grandma wiggles her fingers at me in a little wave. *For Pete's sake, Grandma. I can't wave back. It's a concert. We have to be professional.* I give her a smile, then turn back to my music stand.

I take a deep breath to calm my nerves. For the first time, there's nobody between me and the audience. Nobody blocking me from the spotlight. Nowhere to hide if I screw up.

"Are your parents here, Brie?" Colby whispers.

"Parents and both sets of grandparents." I groan. "What about you?"

"My mom couldn't make it, but my dad is here," he says. He points to where his father is sitting. Next to Colby's dad is Tawni. I look away before she and I make eye contact. I already feel guilty enough that I'm in her seat—I don't want her sad eyes to suck the music out of me.

Marc's friend Paul is always the last musician to take the stage before a performance. He is our principal first violinist, also called the concertmaster.

Paul gets his own round of applause when he makes his entrance. He bows to the audience, then turns to face the orchestra. He plays an A on his violin. The rest of us tune our instruments to match the note he plays.

Paul sits down, and a few moments later Mr. Holmes strides out. He's changed into a tuxedo. He shakes the concertmaster's hand, bows to the audience and takes his place on the raised platform in front of us.

The audience is silent. We musicians have our instruments poised. Mr. Holmes scans the orchestra. He lifts his arms, mouths a silent *One and two and three and...*

* * *

An hour later, it's all over. We join the audience in the lobby for a post-show reception.

Dad films me walking into the room. "Here's our star cellist," he cries, waving his arm like a windmill. "Over here, Brielle."

"Dad, knock it off." I stick out my tongue for the camera.

"How does it feel to be the best cellist in the band?" he asks, not knocking it off.

Mom throws her arms around me. "Brielle, you were fantastic! I am so proud of you!"

I have to admit, I'm pretty pumped about how I performed. I goofed a couple of times, holding notes too long, and I played a wrong note in the Lady Gaga number. My solo was a bit stiff because I was so nervous. Otherwise, it was all good.

That's the whole point of this concert though—to work out those glitches before we play for a *real* audience.

"Not a bad performance this aft, Bum." Marc comes our way, balancing two plates of food. "You didn't embarrass me."

What a nice brother he is, bringing me snacks. I reach for one of the plates.

"Hey, hands off my grub." Marc pulls the dishes out of my reach. He takes off to find a place where he can stuff his face in peace.

"Here, Brielle, have some of mine," says Mom, picking up her plate and frowning at Marc's back.

Before I can lift so much as a cracker, the grandmas and grandpas swarm me. They smother me with hugs, head pats and hair rufflings. "Granddaughter, I had no idea you could play like that," says Grandpa Don. "You brought your grandmother to tears."

They're all beaming. Dad is still recording.

He keeps shooting as Ella and her mom come over to congratulate me. He videos Colby and Grant high-fiving me as they make a beeline for the food tables.

"Dad, stop," I plead.

"Brielle, I'd like a word with you, please." In all the chaos, I didn't see Mr. Holmes approach. *Uh-oh. What now?*

"Yes, sir?" I gulp.

"Brielle, you played beautifully today," he says, smiling. "You proved that you belong in first chair. Congratulations." He reaches out to shake my hand.

I look at Dad to make sure he's still filming. This is the one thing I want on record! Thank goodness he didn't listen to me and shut the camera off.

"Mr. and Ms. Moran, you must be very proud of your daughter," Mr. Holmes continues. He shakes their hands and moves on.

As I watch him go, my eyes stop on Tawni. She's across the room, talking to one of the French horn players. I feel like I should go speak to her. After all, she gave me this pretty ring for good luck. I look at the silver circle on my finger.

"Brielle, I want to get a photo of you and Marc with your mom and dad." Grandma Anna interrupts my thoughts. She herds my parents, my brother and me into the corner, by some flower displays. We smile. She takes about ten pictures.

Then Mom wants pictures of Marc and me alone. After a few shots Colby sees us and jumps into the frame. We all make goofy faces for the camera.

This is the most fun I've ever had at a concert! It's also the most anyone's ever fussed over me at a concert.

I can't believe that a couple of months ago I was terrified of playing principal cello. I thought I would hate being in the spotlight—but I'm loving all this attention!

Out of the corner of my eye, I see Tawni leaving the reception. She's all by herself.

Maybe I should run after her and talk to her. She looks sad though. She would totally drag me down.

Ella and Grant come running over. They want to be in our photos too.

Except for that jerkface Jaron, we have the perfect cello section right now!

Obviously, I am just as good a leader—and as good a musician—as Tawni is.

Maybe her arm won't heal in time for the end-of-the-year concert. I know that's a harsh thing to hope for. But I don't want to give her back her chair. First chair is *my* place now.

Nine

After the Family and Friends concert, Mr. Holmes added a pair of pieces to our repertoire. "The first half of our program needs a boost," he said as he handed out the new pages of music. "It's too short, and it needs something modern between the two classical pieces."

The works he chose for us are from Aaron Copland's *Rodeo*. Copland was an American composer. He wrote *Rodeo* in 1942 for a ballet company. The full *Rodeo* suite has four dances, but we are only playing two of them.

The first one is called "Buckaroo Holiday." I love that name!

"Buckaroo Holiday" takes about seven minutes to play. It has a funny trombone solo, a trumpet solo and a percussion section that sounds like a horse trotting.

The other dance is called "Hoe-Down." It's fast, and it's fun. It's only three and a half minutes long. I smile the whole time we're playing it!

I'm disappointed that neither of the new pieces has a cello solo. But I'm happy to play some new tunes.

At last week's rehearsal, we focused on "Buckaroo Holiday." Today, we're working on "Hoe-Down."

"One more time from the top," says Mr. Holmes. "Channel your inner cowboy or cowgirl! Think about horses and hay!"

He's so goofy sometimes.

"Bum-ba-di-dum, ba-di-dah-di-dah-di-dah-di-di," he sings, demonstrating the tempo he wants. He raises his baton. "One and two and one and two..."

We play right through to the end without stopping. When we finish, someone claps. I squint into the darkened auditorium. It's Tawni! I was so focused on horses and hay that I didn't see her come in.

What is she doing here?

"Good work, cowboys and cowgirls," Mr. Holmes says to the orchestra. "Let's take fifteen before we do a quick run-through of the Lady Gaga piece."

Tawni waves to me.

"Uh-oh," whispers Colby. "Your competition has arrived."

"Shhhh." I swat him playfully on the shoulder. "I'm happy to see her."

"You are not." He places his bow on our shared music stand. "You like being cellist-in-charge. You have no interest in moving your butt out of first chair."

Is it that obvious?

"I feel bad for her, Colby. She's miserable because she can't play." I lay my cello on its side on the floor and set my bow on top of it. "It feels weird that she's out there, and I'm sitting in her chair."

"It's *your* chair now, Brie," Colby says. "You've earned it."

Other orchestra musicians have surrounded Tawni. Everyone likes her and misses her at rehearsals.

"Colby," I say quietly, twisting the shiny silver ring on my pinkie. "What if Tawni is ready to come back? What happens then?"

"Don't worry about it. Look at her arm. It's still out of commission. She won't be back anytime soon." He stands up. "I'm heading to the break room. You coming?"

"In a minute," I say. "I have to say hi to Tawni."

By now Tawni has freed herself from the others and is making her way up the auditorium aisle toward me. I hop down the short staircase to meet her before she comes onstage.

Tawni is smiling, something I haven't seen her do in weeks. She wraps her arms around me. "Bee, 'Hoe-Down' sounds fantastic!"

"Not bad," I say. "It still needs work before we play it at full speed."

"Well," she says, her eyes sparkling, "I can't wait to play it with you!"

"What do you mean?"

"Look!" She holds up her left hand. The cast is gone. Her wrist and thumb are bound in thick, stretchy bandages instead. She still has a splint on her thumb to keep it straight.

"It's still not totally healed," she says, "but my doctor says I'll be able to start playing cello again in a couple of weeks. I can't wait!"

"That's awesome," I say, trying to sound more excited than I feel.

"Because I'll be coming back soon, I asked Mr. Holmes if I could sit in on rehearsals. I want to listen and follow along in the score. I also need to hear his comments to the cello section." She holds up some pages of music and shows me the notes she's made. "I want to be totally ready to pick up where I left off."

She hugs me again. "I am so excited, Bee! We'll have to get together to practice. I've already started studying the new music."

"Wow," I say, still trying to sound happy for her. "That's great news."

It might be great news for Tawni, but it's not great news for me.

Which one of us will get to play principal when she returns?

"Be careful you don't come back too soon, Tawni," I say in my most supportive voice. "Your wrist and thumb are still bandaged."

"Only for two more weeks, I hope," she says. "I've already started doing exercises to strengthen the muscles—like the ones I showed you."

"But if you start playing too early, you might do permanent damage to your hand. You have to watch it. Maybe you should give it more time."

"Don't you want me to come back, Brielle?" Tawni looks hurt. "I thought you'd be happy for me."

"I am. It's just...I mean..."

Mr. Holmes comes along. He interrupts before I put my foot in my mouth.

"How is our long-lost cellist?" he asks, cutting me off. "It's nice to see you, Tawni. I hear you'll be back with us in a few weeks."

"It's not 100 percent for sure," she says. "My doctor says I'm almost ready. She wants me to wait a little while longer, *just to be on the safe side.*"

I leave them talking and head to the break room to find Colby.

I hope the doctor is wrong. I hope Tawni isn't ready to come back anytime soon.

I know that's mean, but it's not fair for her to come back and take first chair away from me.

Especially when our end-of-year concert is only a month and a half away.

In the break room, I find Colby at the water station. He's filling a bottle that looks like a giant sippy cup.

"What did Tawni say?" he asks.

I put my water bottle under the tap.

"She's coming back in two weeks."

"That doesn't mean she's going to take your job," he says. "There's no way Holmes is going to put her back in first chair right away."

"I don't know," I say. "He's pretty happy to see her."

"Brie, don't be such a downer. Tawni hasn't been rehearsing. She doesn't know the new pieces. She'll be stiff and out of practice." He takes a gulp of cold water.

"Tawni has been principal cellist for two and a half years," I say. "I have only been filling in as principal cellist for two and a half months."

"But you're just as good as she is," Colby says. "When are you going to start believing that?"

Mr. Holmes calls into the break room, "Five minutes, people."

"Gotta go!" Colby dashes to the bathroom before we start the second half of rehearsal.

I drift out of the break room and onto the stage. Tawni has returned to her seat in the auditorium. She's writing notes on a page of music.

I drop myself into the chair at the front of the stage—*my* chair. I pick up the cake of rosin and slide it up and down along the horsehair of my bow.

I'm such a lousy friend. Tawni has had a rough time lately, and all I can think about is keeping my butt in this chair.

A good friend would want her to return to orchestra. A good friend would help her get back up to speed.

No matter what I do now, I can't win.

If I help Tawni get ready to perform again, I'll probably lose my place as principal cellist. If I don't help, I'll probably lose my friendship with Tawni.

Ten

awni's hand is still taped up. She can't play yet, but she keeps coming to rehearsals. For the past two weeks, she's been sitting in the house, listening and taking notes. She and I have talked during breaks.

When she walks in today, though, my heart jumps into my throat.

Tawni is carrying her cello! The cast and heavy bandages are gone. Around her wrist is a simple thin tensor bandage. It's wrapped in a way that leaves her fingers and thumb free to move.

For the first time in almost three months, Tawni is here to play.

I don't know what to do. I'm already settled in first chair. As always, I'm seated and prepared before the others arrive—just as Tawni suggested all those weeks ago. Now that she's here, should I move to second chair?

Tawni enters the music room at the side of the stage. She must be looking for Mr. Holmes.

I'm not ready to give up principal position. I was terrified of taking the job at first, but now I love it. I don't want it to end.

A few moments later Mr. Holmes waves to me from the door of the music room. "Brielle, please come to my office," he calls.

This is not fair! Tawni waltzes in here and goes right back to playing principal. After almost three months of hard work, I am going to be bumped back to second.

Tawni and I cross paths onstage. She's coming out of the music room. I'm going in.

"Hi, Bee," she says. "I can't believe I'm finally going to be playing again. It's been forever!"

"Yeah." I force a grin. "Welcome back."

I don't even slow down as I pass her. "I have to go see Mr. Holmes."

"Oh, okay. See you out there!"

* * *

Mr. Holmes sits me down in his office. I feel like throwing up.

"Brielle," he begins, "as you know, Tawni's here, and she's ready to play."

I nod. "I saw her out there."

"Her mother phoned to let me know she's ready to come back," he continues. "I've been thinking about how to arrange the cello section ever since."

I look at my shoes and bite my lip. *This is so unfair.*

"You have been playing very well, but Tawni has always been first cello."

I know where this is going. *Just tell me I'm being bumped back to second chair and get it over with.*

"It was tough, but I've made a decision that we're all going to have to live with," says Mr. Holmes. "I know there will be hurt feelings. I'm going to count on you to be professional about this, Brielle."

I nod again, without looking up at him. A single tear slides from my right eye. *Don't cry. Don't cry. Don't cry.*

"As principal cellist, you'll have to help Tawni get back up to speed. She needs extra practice. I'm counting on you to help her."

Huh? I look up at him. "Are you saying I'm still first cello? Even though Tawni's back?"

"That's exactly what I'm saying, Brielle."

I do my best to look professional on the outside. Inside, though, my heart is turning happy cartwheels!

"As you can imagine, Tawni isn't totally happy about this news," Mr. Holmes cautions me. "But she's a pro. She knows she's out of practice. She's willing to work hard."

He hands me a new seating chart for the cello section. "This is how I want the section organized now that we have six players again. Please have everyone in their new positions for today's rehearsal."

I look at the diagram and groan.

The front line remains the same—me, Colby and Grant, one, two, three, in that order. That's good. No bad news to deliver to those guys.

The back line, though, has been completely rearranged.

Tawni is to sit in fourth chair. She'll be right behind me at the front of the stage. That means Ella will move over one seat into fifth chair. She'll be in the middle of the back row. Jaron has been bumped to sixth. He is *not* going to be okay with that.

"I'll go let everyone know," I tell Mr. Holmes. I want to prove to him that he made the right decision keeping me as section leader.

I'm dreading dealing with Jaron again. On the other hand, I'm almost skipping with happiness. All my hard work has paid off. I'm going to be principal cellist for the end-of-year concert!

* * *

When I make my way to the cello section, I see that Tawni has already settled into fourth chair. I know it's not where she wants to be.

"All I've thought about for three months is this day," she says quietly, "the day I get to play with the orchestra again. I guess I shouldn't have expected that everything would just go back to the way it was before my accident."

Ella has already plunked herself into fifth chair. She's figured out the new seating plan. As always, she's totally okay with it.

The boys have yet to arrive.

"I studied my music, even though I couldn't play," says Tawni. "I visualized all the fingerings and the bowing. I came to rehearsals. I listened to recordings of the pieces we're playing. I'm ready."

Tawni is laying it on pretty thick. I feel bad for her, but enough with the guilt trip. Mr. Holmes made the right decision, keeping me as principal cellist.

"Your left hand is a bit out of practice, that's all," I tell her kindly. "It'll take time to build up your strength again. I'll help you get back on track."

Colby and Grant come onstage together.

"Tawni!" Grant calls. "Are you playing with us today?"

Tawni nods. "Yup."

"Welcome back, fellow cello," says Colby. He high-fives Tawni, then turns his back to her to lay down his cello. He straightens up, still facing away from Tawni. He catches my eye. He holds his hand close to his chest, giving me a secret thumbs-up.

I can almost hear him saying, *I told you so.*

I try not to smile too much. I don't want to rub it in Tawni's face that I'm principal and she's not.

As usual, Jaron is the last to arrive.

"What's going on?" He doesn't even say hello to Tawni. "Ella, you're in my chair."

"Look who's back," Ella chirps, ignoring Jaron's griping. "Tawni's here!"

"Oh, I get it," says Jaron. "The queen has returned." He looks at me and adds, "Doesn't that mean everything goes back to normal, little princess?"

I remain calm. I do not react to Jaron's nastiness. "Now that Tawni's here, Mr. Holmes has a new plan for the cello section," I announce to all the cellists. I hold up the paper diagram to show them. "Jaron, please take your seat beside Ella."

"As if," he grumbles. "Why do I have to move again? I should stay in fifth chair, where I've always been."

Mr. Holmes is walking onstage, ready to start rehearsal.

"Ella, move," Jaron commands.

I smile at Ella and shake my head slightly. She doesn't budge.

Jaron and I are the only cellists who haven't taken our seats. We're staring each other down. It's a standoff.

I lift my eyes to see Marc watching me from his position behind the cello section. He grins and fist-pumps the air with both hands.

I turn to the front and take my seat at the edge of the stage. Mr. Holmes has arrived at the podium. He looks at Jaron, who is still standing with his arms crossed.

"Ladies and gentlemen of the orchestra," Mr. Holmes says, "please welcome Tawni back to our cello section."

All eyes turn our way.

Jaron is still standing there like an idiot. There is only one empty chair left in the cello section. Sixth chair. He has no choice but to sit in it now that everyone is staring at us.

The rest of the orchestra musicians clap their hands or rap their bows on music stands. The percussion section makes all kinds of noise in Tawni's honor.

She smiles and waves to everyone. I turn to face her. She's blushing. "Welcome back," I say cheerily.

"Okay, okay, enough with the celebrations," says Mr. Holmes, laughing. "Take out the Tchaikovsky. Let's get started."

Eleven

"**M**arc, are you trying to kill me? You're supposed to stop at a Stop sign."

"Don't be a backseat driver, Bum. I mostly stopped. If you don't like the way I drive, you can get out and walk to Tawni's house."

"Hard to do carrying a cello," I say. "Just be careful."

I'm lucky that Marc is still excited about getting his driver's license. He jumps at every chance to take the van out—even if it means chauffeuring me around.

"It's decent of you to help Tawni get back up to speed," he says, keeping his eyes on the road.

"It's not like I have a choice. Mr. Holmes says it's my job as principal cellist to make sure she's ready to play in the big concert."

Marc glances in the rearview mirror. He checks his blind spot over his left shoulder and signals a lane change.

"Her playing sounded pretty good to me at rehearsal on Sunday," he says, guiding the car into the left-turn lane. "I stand right behind her in orchestra now, so I hear every note. She still knows what she's doing."

I hate to admit it, but Marc is right. Tawni's playing wasn't at all rusty at Sunday's rehearsal. Even out of practice, Tawni is a better cellist than the rest of us.

"Watch your back, little sister," Marc says with a grin. "Tawni might have her sights set on your solo."

"It would be so unfair if Mr. Holmes gave it back to her," I whine. "It's not my fault she broke her wrist. And I've covered for her the whole time."

The left-turn light turns green.

"Just because she's bummed that she's not the best anymore, it doesn't mean I should have to step down."

Marc presses the gas pedal and turns onto Tawni's street. "Brielle, chill. I'm just giving you a hard time. You're not stepping down. You're still principal cellist."

I take a deep breath in. I let it out slowly. "But what if that changes? What if I help Tawni, and she gets really good again? Mr. Holmes will totally boot me out of first chair."

Marc pulls the van up to the curb in front of Tawni's house. "That's not going to happen."

He's being all big-brotherly again. "You are principal cellist. And right now, that means it is your job to help Tawni improve. Make sure you do that today, kiddo."

I frown at him. I hate being called kiddo more than I hate being called Bum.

"Yeah yeah." I open the door and climb out of the van.

"What time should I pick you up?" Marc asks.

"We're going to practice for an hour or so," I say, figuring out the schedule in my head. "Then Tawni's parents want me to stay for dinner. And we might practice more after that."

"So what time?"

"Probably around seven o'clock. I'll text you when I know for sure."

I haul my cello out of the van. "Thanks for the ride!" I call to Marc as he pulls away—driving too quickly, if you ask me.

Tawni's already at the front door, waiting for me. "Hi, Bee!" she calls, smiling and waving.

By the time I lug my cello up the front walk, Tawni's mother is there too. "Hello, Brielle," her mom says. "Thank you for coming to help Tawni. Though she wouldn't need your help if she hadn't been so clumsy doing that ridiculous balance beam routine."

Tawni's smile fades. She looks away.

"No worries, Ms. Salvo," I say. "I'm happy to practice anytime."

"Tawni," she says sharply. "Don't just stand there. Take Brielle's bag, so she can carry her cello."

"Oh, I'm fine to carry—"

Tawni's mom turns back to me. "The room at the back of the house is all set up for you," she says sweetly. "It will be nice to hear good music in the house again after all these months."

Tawni slides my bag off my shoulder so she can carry it for me. "Come on, Bee. Let's go play."

* * *

This is the first time I've been to Tawni's new house. It's two buses away and a pain in the butt to get to.

Not that she ever invited me to her old house either. Even before her family moved, she and I always hung out at my place. It was closer to school. Plus we had a bigger TV.

I'm guessing that's not true anymore. This house is massive. It's three times the size of their old one. My eyes pop as we pass a spiral staircase and a statue. A statue! Who has a statue in the hallway?

Tawni's music room is at the end of a long hall. And it's amazing. It has a high ceiling and tall windows that overlook the backyard. It is bright and beautiful—unlike the dark basement room where Marc and I play.

"No wonder you love practicing!" I say to Tawni. "I would spend all day in here if I could."

"I love being in here," she says. "Just me and my cello."

Near the windows are two chairs and two music stands. Between the chairs is a small table with pencils, erasers, notepaper, rosin, two glasses and a jug of water.

I unpack my cello and bow. Tawni organizes my music in the order she wants to play the pieces.

"Let's start with the two new Aaron Copland dances," she says. "Those are the ones I need the most help with."

We end up working on "Buckaroo Holiday" and "Hoe-Down" for about an hour. Dinner is still not ready, so we move on to the Lady Gaga piece for a bit of fun before we take a break.

"Too bad Ella's not here!" I laugh.

I count us in, and I sing along. "*Rah rah ah-ah-ah.*"

By the time we get to the chorus, we're both singing at the top of our lungs.

"*O-o-o-o-oo-o-o-o-o-oooo...*"

It's hard to play because we're laughing so hard.

"*Ro mah ro-mah-mah! Ga-ga ooh-la-la!*"

The cello part gets pretty boring toward the end, so we stop singing.

Still, we get a round of applause for our silly performance.

It's Tawni's father. "Very funny, girls," he says with a smile. He's leaning against the music-room door. "Sorry to interrupt your serious work, but dinner's ready."

"Okay, we'll be right there, Dad," says Tawni.

We're still giggling and singing as we loosen the horsehair on our bows and set our cellos on their sides on the floor.

"*Rah rah ah-ah-ah!*" we chant all the way to the dining room. "*Ro mah ro-mah-mah! Ga-ga ooh-la-la!*"

Twelve

"I hope you girls are hungry. We have salad and lasagna—and chocolate cake for dessert."

Tawni's parents have made a huge meal. I wash my hands at the kitchen sink and sit at the table.

"I'm starving, Ms. Salvo!" I say. "This looks delicious."

Tawni's mother places a giant slab of pasta on my plate. Her father passes me the salad bowl. "Go ahead and start eating, Brielle. Don't wait for Miss Slowpoke." Tawni is still drying her hands.

I load a scoop of tossed salad onto my plate.

"Salad dressing, Brielle?"

"Yes, please, Mr. Salvo." He passes me a small jug. I pour the dressing over my pile of lettuce as

Tawni sits down. I don't want to start eating until she's at the table with us.

"You girls play beautifully together," says Tawni's mother.

My mouth is full of lasagna, so all I can do is smile at her and nod my head.

"You've still got it, Tawni," says her dad. "A few more practices, and you'll be right back in that first chair!"

I stare at my dinner plate. *Hello? I'm sitting right here, sir. In case you have forgotten, I'm principal cellist right now. I'm here to help your daughter but not so she can replace me.*

Tawni's mother chimes in. "If only you hadn't been so clumsy on the balance beam, Tawni. I can't believe you made such a stupid mistake. You are never going back to that gymnastics team."

Tawni is sitting across the dinner table from me. She opens her mouth to say something, but her mother keeps talking.

"It's not like you're headed to the Olympics or anything." Ms. Salvo snort-laughs, as if that's funny. "Stick to what you're good at, Tawni. That means playing cello. Period. No more of those silly twirling and tumbling routines."

I shovel salad into my mouth and keep my focus on my plate.

"But Mom," Tawni starts, "that was just a freak accident on the beam. It won't happen—"

"Tawni, your mother is right," says her dad. "You have to focus on the cello. It's your ticket into a university program. Lord knows your grades aren't good enough in your other subjects."

What are they talking about? University is more than three years away for Tawni and me.

He points his fork at his daughter. "You're hopeless at math and science. Music is all you have."

He looks at me. "What mark did you get on your math test last week, Brielle? I'm sure it was better than the B Tawni got. She'll never get anywhere with grades like that."

"Well, ummm," I stutter. I don't want to answer. I don't want Tawni to feel bad that I got a better mark than she did.

"Tawni, sit up straight," her mom butts in, getting me off the hook. "Your posture has gotten lazy without your cello practices. It's time to shape up."

I can't believe how mean Tawni's parents are. This is not the first time I've met them—I've said hello to them at concerts now and then. But this is the first time I've been invited over for dinner. I hope it's the last time. *I wish I could get out of here.*

Thank goodness, Tawni's mom finally changes the subject.

"Brielle, where did you buy your top? It's very pretty."

"Oh, thank you. My grandparents gave it to me for Christmas. They got it at Gigi's Fashion Boutique on Lang Street."

"I'll have to take Tawni there to get her some decent clothes. You'd think we were dirt poor the way the girl dresses." She rolls her eyes. "The only time she looks nice is when she's dressed up for orchestra performances. She always looks glamorous in her formal concert outfit."

Ms. Salvo smiles at Tawni with stars in her eyes. It's the first time I've seen her look at her daughter with anything but a scowl today. Tawni shoots her mom a weak grin.

Ms. Salvo stands up. "You're lucky you have a friend like Brielle who is willing to help you get yourself together, Tawni. Otherwise, you might not get to wear your black and white this year at all." She shakes her head. "As it is, you've dropped to fourth cello. Unbelievable."

"You really blew it this time," says Tawni's dad. He tosses his fork onto his plate. The clatter makes me jump.

"Tawni, clear the plates from the table," says her mom.

Tawni gets up without a word and does as she's told.

Ms. Salvo turns her gaze to me. She claps her hands together, smiling cheerfully. "Who wants cake?"

I had no idea Tawni lived like this. My parents are always proud of Marc and me—no matter what. Even if we get low marks at school, or if one of us plays a wrong note in a concert. Even the time I tripped and fell on my face at a track meet, I knew my mom and dad still supported me.

Poor Tawni. Her parents don't even seem to *like* her, let alone support her.

"We appreciate you taking the time to help Tawni," says Mr. Salvo. "I just hope you can get our little Queen of Clumsy back in shape in time for the big concert."

"Mr. and Ms. Salvo, Tawni is the best cellist in our orchestra. She's probably better than the cellists in the senior orchestra too. She could play that concert today if she had to."

Tawni smiles at me.

"In fact," I continue, "why don't we go practice some more instead of having cake, Tawni? I'm too full to eat one more thing."

"Good idea, Brielle," says Mr. Salvo. "Practice makes perfect!"

* * *

An hour later, I text Marc to pick me up.

While I'm waiting for him, Tawni and I pack up our cellos. "Do you want to practice together again tomorrow?" I ask. "We can go to my house after school, so Marc doesn't have to drive me over here." *And so I don't have to spend any time with your crabby parents.*

"That would be great," says Tawni. "I guess I can take my cello on the bus. I wonder if it costs extra."

"Wouldn't your parents drive you?" I ask.

"I'm not sure," she says slowly. "With their work schedules..."

Unbelievable. They'd make Tawni haul her cello on the bus instead of giving her a lift?

"You know what?" I say brightly. "Marc is on his way over here right now. We'll take your cello with us. It'll be there waiting for you to practice with me after school tomorrow."

"I was going to play a bit more tonight," Tawni says, thinking out loud. "But maybe I don't—"

"Wait, I have a better idea." I interrupt her thought process. "Marc is always looking for an excuse to drive. We'll swing by and pick up you and your cello in the morning."

"It's way out of the way," Tawni says.

"No. It'll be fun. That way, we can walk to school together, just like the old days!"

Marc pulls up to the curb.

"You can even leave your cello at our house, if you want," I say. "We can practice every day after school. Marc will play with us sometimes too."

"But Bee, I thought you could only work with me once a week. You don't have to do any more than that."

"Yes I do," I call to her as I lug my cello down the front walk to the car.

I *have* to help Tawni get back into first chair. It's where she belongs—and it's the only thing that will get her parents off her back.

No wonder she is so devoted to her music. I enjoy playing principal cello, but Tawni *needs* to do it. I'm going to do whatever I can to help her get back on top. Even if it means I'm not cello number one anymore.

Thirteen

For the next three weeks, Tawni and I practice together at least four times a week. We work on every detail of every piece of music.

Sometimes her grouchy parents even drive her to my house, so Marc isn't stuck being her personal chauffeur.

By the time we get to the final orchestra rehearsal before our end-of-year concert, Tawni is back to her brilliant self. Now it's time to convince Mr. Holmes that she should return to the principal cello position—and I have a plan to make that happen!

First of all, I make sure Marc and I are almost late for the rehearsal.

"Brielle, what is up with you?" Marc yells. He's upstairs, ready to leave the house, I'm packing up my cello in our practice room downstairs.

"One of my strings broke. I have to fix it before we leave," I lie. "I'll be right up."

"Well, hurry up." Marc is getting mad. "As principal players, we have to get there before everyone else."

He's right about that. I don't want him to get in trouble. But I want to show Mr. Holmes that I'm not a good role model anymore—meaning I should not be principal cellist.

"Okay, okay." I haul my cello upstairs. "I'm ready. Let's go."

By the time we arrive at the rehearsal hall, most of the other cellists are already in their seats, ready to play. Except Jaron, of course.

"Bee, is everything all right?" Tawni asks. "You're always early. What happened?"

"Everything's fine," I say. "I broke a string."

I unpack my cello, bow and music. "I have to talk to Mr. Holmes before we start."

"You don't have time," Tawni says. "Just sit down. Talk to him later."

Colby gives me a weird look. "What are you up to?" he asks.

"Shhh. Never mind."

I run off the stage and into the music room. Mr. Holmes is leaving his office, coming my way.

"Brielle, nice of you to join us. It's not like you to arrive so late," he says when he sees me. "Being late is not a good quality in a principal cellist."

"That's sort of what I want to talk to you about, sir."

"Talk fast. We need to get going." He walks as we talk.

"I've been thinking about the job of principal cellist," I begin. "Tawni and I have been practicing like crazy for the past three weeks."

"I can tell," he interrupts. "You're playing better than ever. And Tawni's back in top form."

"That's what I think too," I continue. "Tawni has worked really hard, and she's playing better now than she played before her accident. She's the best in the orchestra, that's for sure."

We arrive at the door of the music room. "Plus," I add quickly, "Tawni is always on time for rehearsals."

Before we step out onto the stage, Mr. Holmes stops and looks at me.

"Brielle, what are you trying to say?"

"It's just that...well...I think Tawni should be promoted to principal chair for our concert. It would mean a lot to her." *And to her nasty parents.*

Mr. Holmes adjusts the pile of music in his arms. "Are you getting cold feet, Brielle? You've worked hard too. You're an excellent player, and you've become a strong section leader."

He walks onto the stage. I follow.

"You're right about Tawni's skills though," he continues thoughtfully. "She definitely could play principal again."

He agrees with me—Tawni should be first cello!

Mr. Holmes stops walking. He turns and looks me in the eye.

"But we are not making a major change in the cello section this late in the game, Brielle. First chair is yours. Now, please take your seat."

He strides to his place at the front of the orchestra. I drop into my chair at the edge of the stage. Colby leans over. "What was that all about?"

"Nothing."

Other than the fact that setting a bad example by being late, and reasoning with the conductor, didn't work. I'm still principal cellist—and Tawni is still in fourth chair.

"It's all good." I pick up my cello and bow.

Time for plan B.

* * *

Because this is our last rehearsal before the big concert, we run through our pieces in the order we're going to perform them next Saturday night.

That means we begin today's rehearsal with *The Magic Flute Overture.* It opens with three long, loud chords. It continues slowly and quietly for about a minute. I imagine I'm creeping through a forest during this part. In the middle, it gets quick and darts back and forth between different instruments. It's loud, then quiet. Then it's loud again. Then quiet again. This part makes me think of birds flying all around us in the forest. After that the music becomes more dramatic—and the cello part becomes more challenging. At the end, the Overture is grand and playful at the same time. I know that doesn't exactly make sense, but it feels like a magic spell. It's an exciting opening to our concert program.

Today, as we practice the overture, I notice Mr. Holmes snapping the fingers of his left hand. That means he's pleased with our performance!

After we play it once through, he stops us. "I want to go over the middle section of this piece one more time before we move on," he says. "Let's pick it up at letter D."

Colby and I find letter D in the sheet music we share.

"Focus on your volume this time through," Mr. Holmes continues. "I want to hear a clear difference between the loud and soft parts. It changes quickly, so be precise."

I look around at the rest of the cellists. It's my job to make sure they understand what our conductor is talking about. They all nod. Even Jaron—he wouldn't dare be a jerk this close to a major performance.

"Let's try it again." Mr. Holmes raises his baton. "We'll play from letter D right through to the end."

This time he's happy with our volume, so we move on to the next pieces in our concert program.

We practice the two Copland dances, "Buckaroo Holiday" and "Hoe-Down," a few times. Then we work on my favorite, *Marche Slave*. It will be the last number before intermission at next week's concert.

"Congratulations, musicians," says Mr. Holmes after we play *Marche Slave* perfectly. "The first half of our concert program is in great shape. Let's take fifteen minutes before we work on the second half of the show."

Break time. Time for me to put plan B into effect.

"Great work, cello section," I say to my fellow players. "We rock!"

When they are all looking my way, I stand up quickly. Immediately I drop back into my seat with a thud. *Ouch. That was harder than I meant to fall.*

"Brielle!" cries Tawni.

Colby grabs my arm to keep me from tumbling off my chair. "Are you okay?"

"I'm a bit dizzy," I tell them. "I'm sure I just stood up too fast. I'll be fine. Maybe I need some water."

"I'll get you some," says Ella. She grabs my empty water bottle and runs to the music room.

"You should eat something," says Tawni. "If you're hungry, that can make you dizzy. Here, have this granola bar."

She hands me her snack, but I shudder. I grab my tummy and shake my head. "I don't think I should eat anything right now. My stomach has been upset all day."

Wait a minute. That's a great idea!

"On second thought, maybe you're right, Tawni. Maybe I should eat something. Maybe I'm light-headed because I haven't eaten enough today."

Ella comes back with water. I take a few sips.

"I'm fine now, everyone. Go take a break. I'll sit here for a minute or two and eat my granola bar."

Colby opens his mouth to say something. "Just go," I tell him.

* * *

At the end of the break, Tawni and Ella come and find me—sitting right where they left me ten minutes ago.

"Are you feeling any better?" Tawni asks.

Ella picks up my water bottle. "Do you need more water? I can fill this again if you want me to."

"Thanks, but I'm totally fine now," I tell them. "I don't know what happened, but I'm sure I'll be okay for the rest of rehearsal."

Colby, Grant and Jaron make their way back to the section. Marc is coming over too.

"Everything all right, Bum?" he says on his way to the bass section.

I shoot him a glare. "Don't call me—"

"Can't I be concerned about my little sister? You're not yourself today, kiddo. First you almost make us late for rehearsal. Now I hear that you tipped over during the break."

"It's nothing," I tell him. "But if...ahhh... anything happens during the rest of rehearsal, I'll wait for you by the van."

"What are you talking about?"

Just then Mr. Holmes raps his baton on his music stand to get our attention.

"Settle down, ladies and gentlemen. It's time to look at the rest of our program."

The second half of our concert consists of two pieces—*Mind Over Mountain* by Canadian composer Tobin Stokes, followed by *Capriccio Espagnol.*

That's the piece with the cello solo, and it's the last piece on the official concert program.

We also have an encore number prepared, just in case the audience enjoys the show and wants us to play more. That's where Lady Gaga's "Bad Romance" fits in. We'll practice that number today too.

After we run through *Mind Over Mountain* a few times, we move on *Capriccio Espagnol.*

Time for me to perform again!

Mr. Holmes raises his baton to count us in.

At that moment I grab my stomach and double over in my chair. I groan loudly.

"Brielle!" Colby yells.

Ella shrieks. Tawni jumps up and puts her hand on my back.

Mr. Holmes doesn't move. He looks my way with his mouth open. His baton is still in the air.

I lower my cello to the floor and make a show of gagging. I hold my stomach with one hand and cover my mouth with the other. "I knew I shouldn't have eaten anything," I moan. "I'm going to throw up! I have to get to the bathroom."

I jump up and run off the stage. If I wasn't working so hard at being fake-sick, I'd be laughing my head off at the stunned faces staring at me.

"Tawni will have to play my solo," I yell as I run out of the auditorium.

Fourteen

Marc runs out of the auditorium after me. He finds me in the parking lot by the van. "Brielle, what's wrong? Should I call Mom and Dad?"

"No, go back inside and make sure rehearsal continues. Make sure Mr. Holmes lets Tawni play the cello solo in *Capriccio Espagnol.*"

"What is going on?"

"I'm *sick*, Mark." I make air quotes with my fingers when I say the word *sick.*

He scrunches his face at me. "Brielle, what are you talking about?"

My brother can be so thick sometimes. I sigh loudly. "Marc. It's really important that Mr. Holmes hears Tawni play the cello solo. That's why I'm *sick*—so she has to perform it."

"Little sister, you really *are* sick. What a dumb thing to do. You'll be lucky if you don't get kicked out of orchestra."

"Tawni's parents will hate her if she is not principal cellist in next week's concert. We have to help her!"

Marc crosses his arms and leans on the van. "I see what you're doing, Bum," he says kindly. "But it's not up to you to solve Tawni's problems."

"Marc," I say. "Please. Just go back inside. Make sure she plays the solo. I'll wait here until rehearsal is over."

At that moment the auditorium door flings open. Mr. Holmes runs out into the parking lot. He slows to a walk when he sees us. Tawni, Colby and Ella are right behind him.

"Go back inside, cellists," Mr. Holmes instructs my friends. "Brielle is okay."

They do as he says. They go into the building—but I see their faces watching us through the window.

As Mr. Holmes comes closer, I double over in fake pain again.

"Knock it off," Marc scolds me.

"Thank you for looking after your sister, Marc," says Mr. Holmes. "I'll take it from here."

"Yes, sir. I think she'll live."

Thanks a lot, big brother.

"Please go back inside and tell the other musicians that Brielle is alive and well. Then lead them through the first part of *Capriccio Espagnol.* I'll be in shortly."

He points his chin toward the faces in the doorway. "And take that trio of nosy cellists with you."

"Will do." Marc leaves me by the van with Mr. Holmes.

The conductor looks at me and crosses his arms. I don't make eye contact. Neither of us says anything for a moment.

Eventually Mr. Holmes breaks the silence. "That was quite a performance in there," he says.

"I don't know what—"

"Enough," he says in a stern voice.

I stare at my shoes. After another few painful, silent seconds, he speaks again.

"I trust your sudden illness has passed?"

I force myself to look at him.

"I still don't feel..." I start. Then I stop myself. He knows I'm not sick. There's no point in faking it anymore.

I bite my lip and look down at my hands. "Yes, sir."

"Do you plan to be well enough to play in our concert next Saturday night?"

"Yes, Mr. Holmes. But I really think Tawni—"

He interrupts. "Brielle, I know you want Tawni to play principal cello. You have made that *very* clear—in many different ways."

He shakes his head and chuckles a bit.

"I agree that Tawni is playing as well as she's ever played," he continues. "And when it comes time to audition for next year's orchestra, she can try out for first chair again."

I look away from him, across the parking lot. *But Tawni needs help now, not three months from now!*

"But for today—and for next week's concert— *you* are principal cellist, Brielle," he says. "There can only be one soloist in the section."

"Yes, sir," I say out loud. In my head, though, a brainstorm is brewing.

Mr. Holmes turns toward the auditorium door. "Enough of this. Let's get back inside, Brielle. We have a rehearsal to finish."

And you, sir, have just given me a most amazing idea!

* * *

A week later, Tawni, Marc and I—and all the musicians of the intermediate City Youth Orchestra— are gathered in the music room. After ten months of rehearsals, our final performance of the year is just fifteen minutes away.

Mr. Holmes starts his pre-show pep talk. "This is it, orchestra," he says. "This is the moment we have worked toward since September."

He looks around the music room at all of us dressed in our formal black-and-white concert outfits. "You look fantastic. You play beautifully. Now go out there, enjoy the music, and enjoy your moment in the spotlight!"

We all clap.

Just before we go onstage, I pull Tawni aside.

"I want to give you something," I tell her. "It's for good luck tonight."

I pull the little silver ring off my pinkie and hand it to her.

"No, Brielle, that's yours," Tawni says.

"Tonight, I want you to wear it." I put it in her hand. "I know we're not allowed to wear dangly jewelry when we play," I say, repeating the words she said when she gave me the ring two months ago. "But I think you can get away with a pinkie ring."

She laughs and hugs me.

Mr. Holmes calls to us. "Okay, musicians, pick up your instruments and line up."

As principal cellist, I take my position at the head of the cello section for the walk onstage. We follow Marc and the bass section into the auditorium.

The audience claps as the orchestra makes its entrance.

Mom, Dad and my grandparents are in the front row—as usual. Dad is recording every move that Marc and I make—as usual. This time, I flash a smile for the camera.

I'm excited. This is my first major concert as principal cellist. The Family and Friends performance was a warm-up. This is the real thing.

We remain standing until all the musicians have arrived in their places. As we wait, I notice that Tawni's parents are seated a few rows behind my family. While my parents are grinning and clapping like fools, Ms. Salvo is motioning to Tawni to stand up straight. Mr. Salvo is texting.

Tawni is behind me, in fourth chair, so I can't turn around to give her a smile of support. I'm happy she's wearing my ring for good luck. I hope that when her parents see what we have planned for tonight, they'll be proud of her for a change.

Finally, all the musicians are onstage, so we take our seats. The concertmaster enters. More applause. Last in is Mr. Holmes. He marches across the stage to the podium. He bows to the audience, then turns to face us, baton raised.

"Here we go!" whispers Colby.

* * *

The first half of the concert is perfect. Just before intermission, the audience goes crazy for *Marche Slave*. It's a dramatic finish to this part of the show, and we play it better than we have ever played it before. We get a standing ovation—and we're only halfway through the program!

During intermission Mr. Holmes gathers us for a half-time talk. "I know you're all excited about the reaction to *Marche Slave*," he says in calming tones. "Remember, though, we have another half hour of music to perform. Think about the two pieces we are about to play. Take a few deep breaths. Focus."

Fifteen minutes later we return to the stage. We are settled, poised and ready for Act 2.

The second half of the program opens with a crazy-fast number called *Mind Over Mountain* by contemporary composer Tobin Stokes. He wrote it in 2006 after competing in a series of wilderness adventure races also called Mind Over Mountain. The three parts of the twelve-minute piece—Cycling, Trekking and Paddling—were inspired by the three parts of the race. By the time we've finished playing all three, I feel as if I have run a race!

Luckily, Mr. Holmes gives a little talk to the audience after *Mind Over Mountain*. That gives us time to catch our breath before we move on in the program.

"Ladies and gentlemen," he announces. "We have now come to the final musical number of the evening. *Capriccio Espagnol* is a set of five songs by Russian composer Rimsky-Korsakov."

This is it, the piece with the cello solo. I take a deep breath as Mr. Holmes continues.

"Thank you all for coming this evening. I hope you enjoy our final selection."

He turns to face the orchestra and sneaks a wink at me.

The first song in the *Capriccio Espagnol* set is only one minute long, and it's almost as fast-paced as *Mind Over Mountain*. After that are two more short sections before we come to "Gypsy Song"—the one with the cello solo.

"Gypsy Song" opens with a violin solo, followed by flute, clarinet and harp solos. The cellos and basses don't play during this part of the song.

When the whole orchestra comes in, we pluck our strings in an easy pizzicato. Next, the violin section takes the lead, playing a graceful, flowing melody. The cello solo follows the violins.

I count down to the solo. Five bars to go. Four. Three. Two. One.

Mr. Holmes points his baton in my direction.

In perfect time, Tawni and I draw our bows across the strings. The sound of our two cellos soars through the auditorium.

Ella gasps. Mr. Holmes's head snaps our way. All sorts of expressions cross his face—confusion, anger, even a tiny bit of amusement. He's a pro though. He doesn't let the audience see his reaction.

Tawni and I have played this solo together so many times in the past few weeks that we play it as one. We perform it perfectly tonight, if I do say so myself.

Before we know it, the solo is over. The rest of the orchestra joins us for the end of "Gypsy Song" and for the rest of the piece.

When we play the last three dramatic notes, the audience jumps up and cheers! Mr. Holmes gives me a steely look as he turns around to face the house. He bows, then turns back to the orchestra. He motions to each soloist, one by one, to stand for an individual round of applause.

When he gets to me, Tawni and I stand together. I transfer my cello to my right hand.

With my left, I reach behind me for Tawni. We join hands, face the audience and bow together.

In the front row, my parents and grandparents are going crazy. Mom is jumping up and down. Dad is still shooting video. The grandparents are clapping like mad.

A few rows behind my family, I see Tawni's parents. They, too, are on their feet. Tawni's dad gives her two thumbs up. Her mother blows her a kiss.

Mr. Holmes motions for the whole orchestra to stand and bow. I know he'll lecture Tawni and me after the show for turning the solo into a duet. But it was worth it to see Tawni's parents smiling proudly at their daughter for once.

I don't know what's going to happen next, and I don't know which of us will be principal cellist next year. It might be me. It might be Tawni. Who knows? It might even be Colby.

Right now it doesn't matter. What matters is that Tawni and I played perfectly tonight, and we did it together. Plus, if this is the only time I ever get to sit in first chair, at least my camera-happy dad got it on video!

Eventually, the cheering stops. The audience settles down. We musicians take our seats. Mr. Holmes raises his baton once more—and we play our Lady Gaga encore.

CITY YOUTH ORCHESTRA

Intermediate Concert

Saturday, June 24, 2017

Christopher Holmes, Music Director & Conductor

THE MAGIC FLUTE OVERTURE.........Wolfgang Amadeus Mozart

(1756–1791)

RODEO: TWO DANCES...Aaron Copland

Buckaroo Holiday   (1900–1990)

Hoe-Down

MARCHE SLAVE.....................................Pyotr Ilyich Tchaikovsky

(1840–1893)

~ *Intermission* ~

MIND OVER MOUNTAIN...............................Tobin Stokes

I. Cycling   (b. 1966)

II. Trekking

III. Paddling

CAPRICCIO ESPAGNOL, OP. 34.............Nikolai Rimsky-Korsakov

I. *Alborada* (Dawn)   (1844–1908)

II. *Variazioni* (Variations)

III. *Alborada* (Dawn)

IV. *Scena e canto gitano* (Gypsy Song)

V. *Fandango asturiano* (Fandango)

Acknowledgments

Many people in the Victoria, British Columbia music community helped compose this book.

First, I must thank Pamela Highbaugh Aloni, of the Lafayette String Quartet, for generously sharing her time and musical knowledge—and for sharing her passion for playing cello. Some of her joy has been transferred to the characters in this story.

As I struggled to find a short solo for my young cellist to play, it was Pamela who found the perfect piece—Nikolai Rimsky-Korsakov's *Capriccio Espagnol*. The cello solo in this set of songs was challenging enough to give my cellist the jitters, but not so difficult that she couldn't master it!

In addition to Pamela, I would like to acknowledge Sheila and Susan of the Greater Victoria Youth Orchestra. Together, this trio helped me create an age- and ability-appropriate concert program for my fictitious youth orchestra. Many of the pieces in the book are pieces the GVYO has played in recent years.

Thank you, too, to Victoria composer Tobin Stokes, who allowed my book-bound orchestra to play his 2006 work *Mind Over Mountain*.

Members of the Victoria writing community also contributed to this project. Thank you to my summer writing group—Alexandra Van Tol, Susan Down and Sandra McCulloch—for their brainpower in the early stages of *Strings Attached*.

I'm grateful to Orca Books, particularly to Sarah Harvey, for asking me to contribute to the Limelights series. Finally, a huge shout-out to editor (and brilliant writer) Robin Stevenson for helping me with this book. Her positive energy, her knowledge of character development and story construction—and her cherry muffins— made the process a treat, a rare one-on-one master class in YA writing.

DIANE DAKERS played cello for eight years, until her high school strings program was canceled. She has written numerous nonfiction books for middle grade readers and one nonfiction book for adults. *Strings Attached* is her third novel with Orca Book Publishers. For more information, visit www.dianedakers.com.

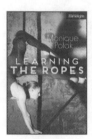

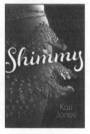

3119202123419